The Junction of Sunshine and Lucky

Holly Schindler

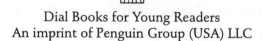

Dial Books for Young Readers
An imprint of Penguin Group (USA) LLC

DIAL BOOKS FOR YOUNG READERS
Published by the Penguin Group
Penguin Group (USA) LLC
375 Hudson Street, New York, New York 10014

USA/Canada/UK/Ireland/Australia/New Zealand/India/South Africa/China
penguin.com
A Penguin Random House Company

Library of Congress Cataloging-in-Publication Data
Schindler, Holly, date.
The junction of Sunshine and Lucky / by Holly Schindler.
pages   cm
Summary: Auggie and her grandfather use found objects to transform the
appearance of their home and, in the process, change a whole town's perceptions
of beauty and art.
ISBN 978-0-8037-3725-9 (hardcover)
[1. Folk art—Fiction. 2. Dwellings—Fiction.
3. Neighborhood—Fiction. 4. Grandfathers—Fiction.] I. Title.
PZ7.S34634Ju 2014   [Fic]—dc23   2013009134

Printed in the United States of America
1 3 5 7 9 10 8 6 4 2

Designed by Nancy R. Leo-Kelly
Text set in Stempel Schneidler

For all the artists who have ever
been told their work wasn't "good."

Old Glory shimmies like she's dancing the jitterbug. That's what Grampa Gus calls his pickup truck, anyway, the one he's always driven, with GUS'S SALVAGE painted right across the doors. She (that's the other thing we've always called the truck, *she*, because Old Glory's a regular part of the family) jiggles so much, she tickles my stomach.

The cab's completely packed—my best friend Lexie's here with me, along with my neighbor Irma Jean. We're in a giant tangle on the passengers' side of the bench seat, our arms and legs weaving in and out of each other as we try to leave Gus enough space to drive.

Our voices sound like a whole playground as we squeal and squirm. Excitement leaks out that way—in shrieks, like air slipping out of a balloon—the day before you get sent to a brand-new school.

"You all are making more racket than a bunch of skeletons break dancing on a tin roof," Gus teases. But the low tones of his laughter tell me that he doesn't

 5

mind at all. I love Gus's belly laugh—it's so hearty, if it were a meal, it'd be chicken fried steak with mashed potatoes and gravy, and pumpkin pie for dessert. So I let a few funny-sounding squeals out on purpose, because I want another serving.

Old Glory inches toward the gates of McGunn's Iron and Metal, a junkyard that Gus knows so well, he could walk through it blindfolded and never once bump his shin on anything. The junkyard stretches on for about fifteen miles. McGunn's takes everything: wrecked cars and old appliances and air conditioners and water heaters. An old plane even calls McGunn's home now, and the wings stand like a giant sloping island in the distance.

A junkyard might sound like an ugly old trash heap, but I've always loved the way the rust at McGunn's makes a pretty orange stripe against the blue sky, right where the earth and the heavens stand back-to-back, making the horizon line.

Gus waves at Mick McGunn, the owner, who has crazy black hair growing all over his arms and out his ears and across his face. It sticks out from under his red ball cap. It pours out from the top of his T-shirt. I wonder, like I do every single time I see him, if it gets tangled in the buttons on his shirts, caught around his watch.

"Got yourselves a real beauty queen there," Mick says as he points to the El Camino attached to the winch on the back of Old Glory.

Mick's right about the El Camino. It's a shell of what it used to be, missing its hood, and its engine, and all its doors. Even its seats and steering wheel are gone now.

But that makes it the perfect car for Gus, who's a trash hauler. Not a garbage collector, like the men who drive giant trash trucks through neighborhoods and pick up weekly bags of sour kitchen leftovers and old waded-up homework assignments. Gus is the guy to call for big jobs. The guy who picks up your broken-down freezers or your junked cars. He'll take your old grills or your rusted patio furniture or even clean out the contents of your grandparents' shed, when they decide they're packing up their house and moving in with you and your parents. He does all of that for a fee, and then brings it to McGunn's, where he trades his hauls for even more scrap money.

It's amazing, I think, his ability to take something broken and worthless and turn it into a fold of green bills in his pocket. Everywhere Gus goes in our town of Willow Grove, people are slapping him on the shoulders, smiling, and thanking him for coming out and hauling off their eyesore of a lawn mower, or asking him to come by again and pick up the swing set their kids have outgrown.

There's something beautiful that happens to people when they get the burden of useless stuff lifted off of them. Their shoulders straighten, and they take fuller breaths, and they smile like they're marathon runners who have gotten their second wind. And that, in my mind, is another special power that belongs to Gus.

We all tumble out of the cab, and Gus steers Old Glory toward a yellow piece of machinery—it almost looks like a bread box built for a giant.

"Here you go," Mick tells us, patting the top of a freezer. "Front-row seats."

Irma Jean is the first to launch herself onto the freezer, flashing a smile as big as her nose—and Irma Jean's nose is enormous.

She's wearing her favorite summer dress, the one with the giant orange flowers and the stretchy top with tiny straps that tie into bows on top of her shoulders. One of Irma Jean's best.

"You're not going to believe what I made for tomorrow," she tells me again, smoothing her sundress down the backs of her legs. "I haven't shown anybody yet. Not even Mom."

"Must be nice to be trusted with the sewing machine," I say as Lexie climbs up on top of the freezer beside us. Irma Jean makes her own clothes out of the hand-me-downs she inherits from her older brothers and sisters. She's so good at it that her mother splurges every now and then on new material—mostly when Walmart has a clearance, less than a buck a yard.

"Your dress will have a hard time looking as good as my new hairdo," Lexie jokes. She can come up with more fancy hairstyles for her long red hair than anyone I've ever seen. Today, a French braid trails straight and thick and strong down the back of her head—like the spine of a book—then spills into a curly ponytail. I wish I could do something fancy with my hair. All Gus and I can ever think to do with the wiry, kinky mess is to tie it into a hundred tiny braids.

As Lexie pats her hair, we giggle. The notes of our giggles are like the notes of a piano chord that have to be played all at once to sound right.

"You all looking forward to the first day of fifth grade?" Mick asks the three of us.

"More than ever," I admit. The idea of it being so close makes my stomach do a little somersault.

"No first-day jitters, Auggie?" Mick presses.

"I've got first-day jitters, all right," I tell him. "But not from nerves. From excitement."

All summer, everyone's been saying "Dickerson," the name of my new school, the same way that they say, "Ooooh. Double chocolate truffle cake." Like it's something they all wish they could sink their teeth into. And a special school is the perfect place for a girl like me to finally find her special-something. Thinking about it makes a smile break out inside me.

The way I figure it, there are two kinds of people in this world—people who shine like the chrome on Old Glory, and people who are more like the rusted metal in McGunn's. My entire life, I've been surrounded by people who shine, who have a special-something. And starting tomorrow, I'm going to find mine.

Gus buys us all sodas from Mick's vending machine, like people buy popcorn at the movies, to have something to snack on while the entertainment unfolds. Irma Jean and Lexie both start guzzling their sodas and swinging their legs from the freezer's edge.

I'm still standing, quietly sipping my soda, as Mick uses a bulldozer with a claw to grab the El Camino through the windows, feed it into the enormous yellow car crusher.

The masher lowers, squeezing the car. At first, the

car looks like it's trying to fight back. But it's no match for Mick's crushing machine. The windshield pops, making tiny glass pieces fly like drops of water from a stomped-in puddle.

Lexie and Irma Jean cheer as if they've just watched a movie villain get his comeuppance. The old El Camino keeps shrinking as the roof is pushed down to the floorboards. Irma Jean and Lexie hoot, clapping. They love these shows.

I have to admit, it really is pretty amazing, watching something as big as a car get turned into a patch of metal that stands about as tall as a concrete block. But today, I can hardly even concentrate on the show. I'm too busy imagining what it will be like to start a new school and discover my shine.

That very night, a monster roars, pressing his bright yellow eye against my bedroom window. He roars again, louder this time, as fiery slime drips from his jaws. He grips my house with his big meaty hands and shakes it, then kicks the boards right above the foundation.

It's late at night—so late, it almost doesn't seem

possible for the clocks in the house to be awake enough to keep track of the time.

I sit up in bed and grab my quilt with my sweaty hands. I scream, my voice every bit as forceful as a punch. I scream again, like maybe it's possible for my scream to beat the monster back.

But the monster isn't afraid of me; he roars even louder, blowing his foul breath into my room and making my first-day-of-school dress, hanging on the closet door, sway back and forth.

I don't know what wakes Grampa Gus, my scream or the monster's growl. But he comes racing into my room, his face ashy and gray with terror. He grabs my wrist and leads me down the stairs. We've got to get someplace safe—we need a tight little hiding spot.

I try to head for the hall closet Gus always keeps locked. But as soon as I put my hand on the doorknob, Gus stops me. "Not there," he says. He wraps his arms around me and steers me toward the hearthstone of the fireplace—the exact center of the whole house. I know Gus feels safer here, but I'd much rather have a nice thick door between me and that awful monster.

"It's all right, Little Sister," Gus whispers into my ear. It's a goofy nickname, since I'm nobody's sister at all.

But coming from Gus, the name always feels like a kiss on the forehead.

"It's just a storm," he murmurs.

Just a storm? Does he really expect me to believe that? It's a monster, and he's kicking and smacking and yanking on our house.

"You know what a storm is, right?" Gus asks, like I'm some little kid. "Just hot and cold clashing. Cold wanting to move in, and warm wanting to hang on for life. See, nothing in this world likes the idea of coming to its end. Not a flower, not a man, and not a season. That's all this is. Summer not wanting to die. And fall trying to push summer on out."

I tremble, because I swear, our house is perfect. And it's taken my whole life to get it that way. We've got a flat, smooth, perfectly round circle in the middle of the living room throw rug that Gus and I have worn thin by dancing. And the glossiest newel post in the entire neighborhood, because we both grab hold of it as we start to climb the stairs. And a hundred other one-of-a-kind markings that I always notice every time I come home.

"You and I," Gus says, "we can ride out any storm."

But I don't want to wait for it to pass.

The monster rattles our screens, taunting us with his strength as Gus stares through the window at the small metal outbuilding in the backyard where he keeps all his old welding equipment. Even though I know it wouldn't work, I keep imagining how great it would be if Gus would turn on that torch, let its fiery breath rush out, and scare the monster so bad, he'd go running away like a scolded dog.

I press my face deep into Gus's chest and tremble against the winds that feel strong enough to turn the entire world upside down.

··· 3 ···

Once I hear the storm monster begin to stomp away, I relax in Gus's arms. I fall asleep to the sound of his heartbeat, and wake up in my room to the sounds of chirping birds. Hard to believe, as I crack my eyes, that my house looks so much like it did yesterday—not flipped upside down by the storm after all.

I put on the dress I've saved for the first day, a sundress with a giant ruffle around the neck instead of a collar. The material—a pinkish-purple that's the same color as my can't-wait feeling—rustles about my knees as I clomp down the stairs, straight for Gus's first-day-of-school buttermilk pancakes.

I wolf down the last maple syrup–drenched bite and grab my new backpack, which feels lighter than a backpack ever should, since it only has my lunch inside it. No math or spelling books yet.

"Come on, Gus! Let's go, let's go!" I shout, racing down our front walk. I'm putting my backpack into the cab of Old Glory when Irma Jean comes running from the house next door. She's only one of a whole crowd, since she's the fifth of eight kids named alphabetically: Anna Beth, Cody Daniel, the twins Ernest Francis and Gertrude Hannah, Irma Jean, Kelly Lilith, Michael Nicholas, and Opal Patricia.

"Well," Gus sighs, like he always does anytime he sees all the Pike kids together, "I guess when Mr. and Mrs. Pike get to the end of the alphabet, we'll know for sure that their family won't get any bigger."

Since Opal Patricia's a baby—all soft coos in a blanket—and Michael Nicholas is barely walking, since Kelly Lilith goes to preschool, Anna Beth and Cody Daniel go to high school, and the twins go to middle school, Irma Jean is the only one of all the Pikes who will get sent to Dickerson with me.

Mr. Pike gives Irma Jean a good-luck hug. It's a little hard for Irma Jean to wrap her arms all the way around her dad, since he has a stomach as round as

15

a large pizza. But her mom is the opposite—so tall and stretched-out, she always reminds me of a giraffe reaching for the tastiest leaf at the top of a tree.

Irma Jean races to our gravel driveway, turning circles to show off her own first-day dress—it's green plaid, with a brown corduroy vest. I can tell she's made the vest from her brother's old coat—but only because I know she had to fight with Cody Daniel to give up his too-small but still-favorite jacket. She looks really studious, like a girl who should be on a poster for the library.

"Loveyourdress," I say. I know my mouth has brakes somewhere, but I can't find them. So my words keep racing forward. "Comeonlet'sgo. WegottapickupHarold."

Gus revs the engine, chanting, "Come on, now, Old Glory," while the truck sputters and threatens to die. "Come on, sweet girl," he pleads, while he strokes the dash like she's really a cat. "Come on, you can do it."

After a few extra sputters and lunges, Old Glory kicks into gear and lurches down the street. With the exception of some tree limbs lying in the middle of a few front yards and leaves scattered across the curbs and streets like confetti after a parade, the neighborhood hasn't suffered much damage at all. In fact, the raindrops that haven't dried up yet make the neighborhood glitter in the sun.

We amble through the streets of Serendipity Place, passing by the Widow Hollis's house. Just like it happens every time I get close to her home, my mind fills with the image of the beautiful irises that bloom in her yard every spring. I'm convinced the only place you'd ever see a blue as deep as her flowers is the bottom of the ocean.

And when Old Glory slows a bit up by Mrs. Shoemacker's place, I swear, yet again, that there can't be grass that thick and beautiful anywhere else—it's as soft and plush as carpet in a movie star's house.

At Ms. Dillbeck's house, I notice that her front porch has weathered so many rainstorms, the boards sag in the middle and curl up at both ends. I think that old porch looks like it's smiling.

I'm glad that silly monster of a storm didn't hurt any of the other homes in my neighborhood, either. Because now that I think about it, pretty much every house in Serendipity Place is perfect. Even the names of the streets. Who couldn't be happy living like Gus and I do, on the corner of Sunshine and Lucky? And one block away, Weird Harold Bradshaw and his dad live in the house Harold's dad grew up in, on Joy Boulevard. Gus and I are so close to Joy, our backyard actually butts up against Harold's, so that we share a fence and a forsythia bush that's planted right smack on the dividing line.

When Old Glory shimmies to a stop, I stare at the enormous gardens Weird Harold and his dad have grown right in their front yard. Late summer squash and bush beans and watermelons and tomatoes are fat and swollen from the sun. Beetle traps buzz and giant rain barrels sit at the ends of the gutters on both sides of the house.

Mr. Bradshaw walks Harold to the truck, smiling all the way—probably because Harold is grilling him again about the gardens. He seems to love how Harold has streamlined their vegetable growing.

"Remember to put my fertilizer on the tomatoes today," he tells his dad. "And with that storm last night, there's no need to water the squash we just planted. . . ."

Weird Harold Bradshaw is super-smart. Scary smart. He's always outdoing everyone at science fairs (last year, he invented a brand-new fertilizer that he and his dad now use on their gardens), and winning spelling bees and history trivia contests. He watches the news because he wants to, not because his dad makes him, and he reads the *Wall Street Journal,* and sometimes, he uses words so long, I think I could jog around the block and back before he gets finished pronouncing them.

When the teachers at our new school get wind of him today, they'll all gasp and huddle close together, their voices quick and excited.

Now, though, Harold climbs into the cab, smooshing Irma Jean and me closer together. And Mr. Bradshaw puts his palms against the driver's side door of Old Glory, nodding a thank-you at Gus for driving Harold to school.

"You know, Auggie," Mr. Bradshaw confesses as his eyes land on me, "you look more and more like your mom every time I see you. One of these days, I'll tell you about all the good times your mom and I had when we were kids. When you're old enough to hear those stories, anyway," he adds, tucking his long gray hair behind his ears as he dissolves into a wheezy laugh.

I smile, act like I'm looking forward to it, but I actually stopped waiting for a story about my mom from Mr. Bradshaw long ago. He's been telling me for years that they were great friends, but he always suddenly has something he's late for when I ask him for any details. I'm pretty sure they didn't share so much as a stick of gum.

I slap the dash. "Come on, Gus," I say. "Dickerson's waiting."

As soon as Old Glory turns into the Dickerson Elementary drive—a long paved tongue that's as jammed, this morning, as a five-lane highway—I see the satin-shiny red hair that's been part of my life since the first grade. Lexie. She's up at the end of the drive, next to the building. Waiting for me.

"Better go, Little Sister," Gus says with a wink. "Catch up with your friend. I'll get out of this jam somehow." He shakes his head at the crazy jumbled-up mess of cars ahead.

Irma Jean and Weird Harold climb out right along with me. I've barely even taken the first step toward Lexie when Harold grabs hold of my arm.

Looking at him, I finally realize Weird Harold's really worked up about something, so much so that his Hawaiian print shirt is buttoned wrong. His glasses have greasy smears across both lenses. I'm not really sure how he can see through them. His blond hair sticks out crazily from a yellow baseball cap, which says AS SEEN ON TV and sits at a crooked slant on his head.

"Dad told me not to mention it—and I didn't want to say anything in front of Gus. But did you see this story?" Weird Harold asks, pressing a torn-off strip of newspaper into my hand.

The newspaper is blurred with Harold's sweat. Whatever the story's about, I'm sure Harold's going to believe it's a plot to ruin the world. Which is exactly why Harold got the "weird" stuck in front of his name. Sure, he's smart—smart enough to convince me he could have whipped Einstein at *Jeopardy!*—but Weird Harold, as everybody's been calling him straight to his face for the better part of the past two years, has a tendency to believe that nothing is as it seems. He was convinced that our old principal at Montgomery was keeping a file on him, monitoring the books he checked out in the school library. And he swears that the Fill 'N Sip two blocks away from his house overcharges him for his ICEEs because, as he puts it, "I'm a kid. Nobody listens to kids."

Gus calls him a conspiracy junkie.

I glance down at the headline. The blurry bold print says something about licensing bicycles. I shrug. I'm so focused on meeting up with Lexie and hurrying inside Dickerson that I don't really think I have the patience for one of Harold's theories.

"We have to pay for the licenses, Auggie," he insists. When he talks, his crooked teeth remind me of a picket fence that's been hit by a tornado.

Irma Jean widens her eyes, points her index finger to the side of her head, and makes tiny circles. *Weird Harold is cuckoo.*

"That's discrimination against kids," Harold says. "It's going to take a month of my allowance to pay for my license. And who rides bikes? Huh? Kids, that's who. Discrimination. Against. Kids."

"Your dad rides a bike," I say, shrugging again. He does, too—even to work every day.

"Listen to me, Aug. Dad's the exception. They're coming after kids," Harold says. "They are. I mean— what's next?"

We giggle, me and Irma Jean, and even though it doesn't quite sound like the laughter I've always made with Lexie—the musical laughter that only happens between two best friends—it's still nice. We break into a jog, straight for the front doors, where Lexie stands.

"Hey!" Harold shouts. "Wait!"

"Lexie!" I call, racing toward her, my nearly empty backpack flopping against my backside. Even from a distance, I can tell she's wearing a French braid that starts high on the right side of her forehead and swoops down across the back of her head, swirling up again toward her left ear. That braid looks like a giant horseshoe, with the ends pointed up to hold all the luck in. She's twisted the ends of her braid into a perfect bun on the left side of her face, and her bangs lay across her forehead in one swooping, thick, beautiful curl.

I can't wait to tell her how amazing it all looks. But when I catch up to her, I realize she's already talking to someone else—a pretty girl our age who looks all dressed up, even in a pair of jeans and a white top.

"I'm Victoria," the girl says as she tosses her hair over her shoulder. As perfect and silky as it lays down her back, I'm sure that Victoria gets it straightened in a beauty parlor.

"Victoria Cole," the girl presses.

"Auggie Jones," I say, realizing she was waiting for me to introduce myself.

"Auggie?" she repeats, to make sure she got it right. She looks over my shoulder, toward the jumble of cars in the drive. "Who brought you?"

"Grampa Gus."

"Gus?" she repeats.

"They're both named August," Lexie volunteers. "Their name got shortened down differently."

23

I sneak a glance at her, realizing what a goofy smile Lexie has on her face.

"That's—sweet," Victoria finally manages, in a way that sounds like she doesn't really believe it's sweet at all.

I guess it's not the prettiest name for a girl, *Auggie*. But that's what happens when your mom's wild. She gives you a man's name—August—and she shortens it down, cuts it with a pair of scissors so that it's stubby and awkward, like a haircut done by somebody's five-year-old sister.

"What's your middle name? Mine's Elizabeth." She rolls her eyes like it's the worst name in the whole world.

"Walter," I say.

"Come on. Really."

"Walter," I say again.

"Walter," Victoria repeats, flicking her long hair behind her other shoulder.

"Her mom named her after her grampa," Lexie jumps in. "First *and* middle names."

"But Walter?" Victoria looks at me like baby snakes have hatched inside my head, and they're all crawling out my nose and ears.

Lexie snickers.

I feel my whole body run cold. Lexie *snickered*?

My mouth feels loose, like I can't get a tight enough grip on any word to say it out loud. As I look at Victoria, my life story rings inside my head like an out-of-tune mandolin. I don't want it to sound bad, the story. I don't want Victoria to think that Mom named me after Gus because she knew that he wouldn't give up on a little innocent baby with his own name. Or that Mom probably didn't even look close enough to know if I was a boy or girl, anyway. Just slapped a name on me and hightailed it out of town, like the wild woman that everyone always says she was.

It crosses my mind that maybe I could make it sound kind of glamorous. That I could tell her I was left on my grampa's doorstep, like in some fairy tale.

I glance over at Lexie. Why isn't she sticking up for me?

"Bet you're glad you don't have to go to that crummy old Montgomery anymore," Victoria says, wrinkling her nose. "My dad's on the school board, and he said that it would have taken a fortune to fix it up right. All leaky and cracked."

The way she talks stings—sure, I know that the school board decided to save money by shutting down Montgomery, where Irma Jean and Harold and Lexie

25

and I all went to school last year. Instead of fixing up the pieces that had worn out on the oldest school in town, the school board redrew district lines and sent some Montgomery students to Eastwood Elementary, some to Rutherford Elementary, and all of Serendipity Place and part of Lexie's neighborhood (which is a block north of mine) to Dickerson. But the way Victoria crinkles her nose, you'd think Montgomery was infested with rats and roaches, ready to fall in any minute.

"What's your grampa do for a living?" Victoria asks, looking past my shoulder again. I follow her squint, realize she's staring right at Old Glory.

My thoughts start flipping back and forth, like fingers searching the pages of a textbook for a decent answer. A way to spin what Gus does into something that sounds far more impressive than it is. I'm not quite sure why I feel this way, though. I've never felt like I had to polish up what Gus does. I've always thought it was pretty amazing all on its own.

"He's a trash hauler," Lexie blurts. It's true, but somehow, her words kick me in the gut.

"A trash hauler?" Victoria whispers, eyeing me sadly. The way she looks at me makes my skin feel itchy.

I think about the shed behind our house, the one

that holds Gus's dusty old torches. When Mom was my age, Gus was a welder. It's always seemed like a wonderful job to me, Gus with his enormous fiery torch, fusing the whole world together.

But I have a feeling Victoria wouldn't be impressed by welding, either.

"He works for himself," I say, the way Gus always does. I don't mention the part about him now being too old to weld all day. "Gus goes out to people's houses and he fills up the bed of his truck with the things that don't quite suit them anymore." Sweat drips from underneath my arms as I ramble on. "He picks up old water heaters and worn-out couches and broken-down stoves and busted-up tables. Last year, he even saved up enough to buy a winch. That way, he was able to pull rusted cars out of rivers where they got abandoned."

Victoria's eyes swell, like she could cry any minute. "You guys get by on that?" She puts her hand to her chest like she thinks someone will have to adopt me and Gus before Christmas, because it's the only way we'll get our stockings filled with nice new things that smell like department stores and plastic wrappers.

"He gets security checks," I say, because these words are powerful in our house. But I can tell, from Victoria's blank stare, that this idea is really as big of a mystery

27

to her as it is to me. Victoria's dad is surely a doctor or lawyer or somebody's boss.

"Aren't you cold in that?" Victoria asks, eyeing my sundress. "You do have fall clothes, don't you?"

I flinch. She doesn't think I have fall clothes? I look to Lexie, but she's too busy smiling up at Victoria to notice that the new girl's words have punched me in the face.

"There goes my dad," Victoria blurts, waving goodbye to a man in a glistening black car. "He's a member of city council, and this morning, he said he's making *me* a junior member of—"

"Wait," Weird Harold butts in. "Did you say the city council? A junior member? I've got to talk to you about these licensing fees," he says, pushing the newspaper strip into Victoria's face.

Victoria's eyes grow large as Harold rattles on, getting so worked up, his glasses flop down to the end of his nose.

"This is wrong," he insists. "The next thing you know, the council is going to make *kids* get licenses, like dogs. They'll make us put chips in our necks so they can keep track of us twenty-four/seven!"

Victoria cocks her head to the side and laughs. Her laughter has such sharp edges, I get the feeling that just by laughing, Victoria's making fun of him. And it hurts me—because I get the feeling that by making fun of Harold, she's making fun of me, too.

··· **5** ···

Right off the bat, our teacher, Ms. Byron, flitters around the classroom in a halfway-panicked way, like a hummingbird that's beginning to think it'll never find its way out of a garage. She chews on chalky stomach pills, so that when she announces, "Please stand for the first Pledge of the year," she looks like she's licked an entire blackboard clean.

As I stand, my eyes rove out across the classroom. Dickerson has that new construction smell of paint and plaster and wood, and our classroom has a marker board instead of a chalkboard and fancy plastic desks and even a projector that's actually hooked to a computer on Ms. Byron's desk. What really gets me, though, is the coatrack. It's crammed with backpacks branded with designer names. And lunch boxes—brand-new plastic lunch boxes, not like the brown paper bags that Irma Jean, Weird Harold, Lexie, and I have brought with us.

I glance through the window at the playground, which is filled with swings and monkey bars that don't have a single scuff mark. And it's dotted with the tiniest little trees you ever saw. Nothing more than saplings, really. It's all pretty, I think. Even the skinny saplings. There's a kind of gentle, fragile sweetness about a baby tree, same as there is for a puppy or a fuzzy yellow chick. But something's missing. I can't quite figure out what, yet. But it makes me start to miss Montgomery, in a way I never thought I would.

After the Pledge, Ms. Byron tells us to grab a partner. "Any partner," she says. "Hurry, hurry," she shouts, her nervousness spewing out everywhere. "For our getting-to-know-you first-day assignment!"

Before I can turn to whisper at Lexie, her chair screeches on the floor—away from me. I feel like the whole world has tilted in that moment. Lexie's desktop thunks against Victoria's. Inside my chest, my heart makes a sound like a piece of paper being torn in half.

When I finally look up, away from Lexie's red horseshoe-shaped braid, I see Irma Jean pointing from her chest to mine.

I nod, trying to pretend that getting Irma Jean for a partner isn't a disappointment. She's a nice girl, Irma Jean. And she can sew like nobody's business. But we've never been best friends. It happens that way, most times. The people who live right next door never seem as interesting as the ones who live a mile away.

As we scoot our desks together, it gets hard to breathe. All the reasons for missing my old school keep piling higher, faster. I decide right then to only miss three things. If I just let myself miss three, I tell myself, maybe it won't sting so bad:

1. I miss the way the old wooden seats were all worn shiny, like they'd been given extra coats of varnish. But it wasn't some coat of glop on those seats. It was that they'd had so many kids sliding in and out of them, to recess and lunch and gym class. We'd buffed those seats with our backsides.

Every Monday morning, as we said the Pledge of Allegiance, I'd look down at the glossy wood of my desk chair and imagine the faces of everyone who sat there before me. Generations and decades of them— even Grampa Gus himself. So many of them, if you piled our yearbooks on top of each other, they'd stretch all the way to heaven.

2. The playground trees. Those trees were so big, any one of them could have made an umbrella for the giant in *Jack and the Beanstalk*.

3. Lunchtime. I loved the way that everybody used

to bring brown bags filled with last night's supper stuck between two pieces of bread. Whatever was left—green beans or a pork chop or tuna casserole. Tastes of home smashed right between two pieces of white.

· · · 6 · · ·

By the time the final bell of the day rings, it becomes pretty clear that Ms. Byron hasn't just been hit with a case of first-day nerves. She's naturally nervous, the same way some people have naturally curly hair or are natural-born swimmers.

She races outside with all of us, flittering about as she tries to help usher her new students toward their parents' cars, waving at the parents in a flurry of after-noon introductions.

Harold, Irma Jean, Lexie, and I cluster together on the sidewalk. At the far end of the front drive, I see her: Old Glory. My face breaks into a smile, because I think, *Here's Gus and here's Old Glory, and look, she's even got a new car attached to the back of her now, an old Toyota, all bashed in on one side. We're going to take it straight to McGunn's, and we'll turn that banged-up, wrecked car into money. Into a piece of metal that's only as thick as a triple-*

cheeseburger. Finally, a little slice of something fantastic.

Harold sees the Toyota and he starts cheering, "McGunn's!"

I smile because Harold, the smartest kid in our class, sees how incredible Gus's job is. And I think that surely, with all of us—Harold and me and Lexie and Irma Jean—screaming and carrying on, Victoria will realize she ought to be impressed, too.

Instead, Lexie takes a step away from us. She calls, "See you tomorrow, Auggie!"

"Wait," I say. "You're not coming to McGunn's?"

"Victoria's giving me a ride!" she shouts.

The two of them race toward Victoria's fancy car, while I stand there in a dress that doesn't look like fall; with Weird Harold, who sees crazy conspiracies even when there aren't any; and with the girl who lives next door, who sews her own clothes out of hand-me-downs.

Victoria swings open the back passengers' door of her father's car, and her mouth droops as she points toward the end of the drive. Toward Old Glory, dragging an awful, terrible-looking car. Other new classmates follow, their mouths drooping at the rusted, wrecked pile of garbage that Gus is dragging up the drive.

Right then, Old Glory looks about a hundred years

older than the cars at Dickerson—she's shaped differently, with her fat fenders, and she growls and clanks louder than all the rest of the cars put together. I cringe at the sight of the winch and the job box propped across the bed and the word *salvage* on the door.

At that moment, as I stare at Victoria, her skin seems the same shade as imported chocolates. When I look down at my legs, beneath the hem of my sundress, my skin looks like ordinary old mud.

No—not ordinary. I was ordinary at Montgomery. At Dickerson, I'm the girl from the poor neighborhood who doesn't have fancy new clothes, and who lives with her grampa the trash hauler.

Old Glory honks to get my attention. Gus calls out, "So how was the first day?"

I don't want to show any hurt feelings in front of him, so I smile wide, like I'm trying to show off a trip to the dentist.

When Gus sees that smile, he cocks his head to the side and sighs. "Come on—climb in," he tells me. "I've got something I need to show you."

As Old Glory slows down a few blocks away, I realize last night's storm sank its monstrous teeth into the Hopewell Community Church. Our church looks like a piece of white angel food cake with a giant bite taken out of it. The steeple hangs, broken. Shattered stained glass from the enormous windows glitters across the parking lot.

My stomach feels yanked—the same way those trees around Hopewell must have felt when their roots were pulled right out of the ground. Crisscrossing power lines are draped like useless, broken rope across nearby car roofs.

"Went to Sunday School there when I was a boy," Gus mutters. "Got married there. Baptized your own mother there. Had your grandmother's funeral there."

Tiny groups cluster on the sidewalk, staring at what's left of our little white church. Women are huddling close, blowing into Kleenexes. They rub each other's shoulders and shake their heads.

I watch how everyone stands back from the old church—like it's a dead body or something. A dead body with a white sheet draped across it. The only one who's close to the church is the minister.

Even from a distance, I can make out the black canvas and white leather toes of his high-tops—the shoes he always wears because his name is stamped right there on the ankle: Chuck Taylor. Chuck says he also wears them because they're like the strings people tie on pinkie fingers to remind themselves of something. And what the Reverend Charles V. Taylor (Chuck for short) wants to remember most are the back alleys his feet used to linger in when he was a real troublemaker. He says remembering those times makes him a better minister.

Gus always tells me it happens that way sometimes. The wildest kids can grow into the straightest and narrowest adults.

Even though Chuck is wearing his same old shoes, there's nothing usual about the scene at all. He stands in front of the crooked front door, shaking his head and rubbing his chin like he knows he needs to go in, if only he could get up enough courage to do it.

I know exactly how he feels as I sit in worn-down Old Glory, with an awful wrecked car attached to her, on our way to a junkyard filled with trash, and with a whole year at Dickerson stretched out before me.

Courage, I think as I stare at Chuck, can sometimes be like when you're dying for a peanut butter and jelly sandwich, but there's only a skiff of peanut butter left on the side of the jar, and no matter how much you scrape, you begin to wonder if you'll ever get enough on your knife to cover an entire slice of bread.

···**7**···

The first Saturday after school starts, Lexie and I circle our bicycles in and out of each other on the sidewalk below the old billboard that can be seen high against the sky almost anywhere you plant your feet in Willow Grove. Our wishing spot, that's what we've always called it.

The old ad for the dress shop is faded now, ripped in places. A giant black sticker with AVAILABLE and a phone number covers a big section in the middle. But I can still see the face of the woman on the billboard, still see that she has her head thrown back, her mouth open like she's in the middle of laughing. Like whoever took that picture caught her in some joyous moment. And I can still see that she's beautiful.

I know that the woman on the billboard is my mother. Gus has told me so, a hundred different times. Gus, and everybody else in Willow Grove. It was my mom's special-something: she was beautiful.

Shining brighter than any star. That's what everyone always says about my mom, that she's off somewhere incredible, like California, shining brighter than any stars out there—the ones twinkling in the sky or on the silver screen.

Which is why her picture has always felt like the most natural place for me and Lexie to put our wishes.

"What're you going to wish?" I ask Lexie. "I'm going to wish that we could all go back to Montgomery."

"What for?" she asks, her nose crinkled.

"Don't you miss it?" I ask. "I wish I could open my eyes and find out that a desk with my name across the front of it has been waiting for me there, all this time."

Lexie shrugs, rustling the waves of her hair that she's letting spill across her shoulders today. "I don't miss it so much. If we hadn't gone to Dickerson, we never would have met Victoria."

I nod, pretend that I've been glad to share Lexie, but I have to admit, the past week has felt a little crowded because of Victoria. She's always around—at lunch, during recess. And even though I try to find things about her to like, there's something about her—I can't quite put my finger on it yet—but for some reason, she reminds me more of a parent than a kid. Maybe it's the way her shirts are always ironed and color-coordinated with her socks, or the way she never has any Band-Aids on her knees. Or maybe it's the way she's always sitting in class with her feet crossed and her chin in one hand, all prim and proper.

"I have to go," Lexie says.

"Where?"

"I have this thing I'm doing with Victoria," she says.

When my face falls, she explains, "I'd invite you, but it's kind of a two-person thing."

"Oh," is all I can manage.

And like that, she lifts her backside from the seat, standing up to get more leverage. She peddles extra-quick, down the street, out of sight.

I grab a notebook from the metal basket on the back of my bike. "Dear Mom," I scribble, because I sometimes write letters to her—even in my head when I have something to say and no paper around.

Today, I feel ready to ask her to come back. Because she's glamorous, that's what everybody says. So glamorous, anyone could tell just by looking at her that she'd spent years floating around on one of those inflatable mats in a movie star's swimming pool, sipping big drinks full of umbrellas, smiling her enormous smile.

I'm still sitting on the curb, staring at my unfinished letter, when a pair of black-and-white high-tops stops on the sidewalk in front of me.

When I turn my eyes up, they land on the face of the Reverend Charles V. Taylor.

"Hello, Auggie," he says, seeming honestly happy to see me.

"Reverend," I say, forcing a smile and nodding once.

"I thought you and I were on a first-name basis," Chuck complains.

I have to admit, it really is a pretty formal thing to call a minister. Most other churches around call their ministers "pastor" or "brother." But I always figured it kind of showed how much we all respect Chuck—even if he does always wear sneakers to church.

He tilts his head, says, "I don't think I've ever seen you at the wishing spot without Lexie."

I hug my notebook to my chest, as though I can cover the wound inside my heart. What I really wish is that friendship didn't have to be so slippery, so hard to keep hold of.

Chuck squints at me a good long while, like he's thinking something over, as Mom's billboard looms behind his shoulder. He follows my gaze, up toward her old picture. "She was my best friend, you know. And I sure do miss her, now that she's gone."

"Seems like there's one person who does the leaving, and one person who does the missing," I blurt.

He lets the tiniest hint of a grin crack into the side of his face. "I never did tell you about the snake, did I?"

I shake my head no.

Chuck's grin grows like a flower blooming on fast-forward. "Then I'll tell you as I walk you home."

· · · 8 · · ·

"Your mom and I sure were troublemakers back when we were younger," Chuck reminds me as we head back toward the giant brick sign, branded SERENDIPITY PLACE. "That's what everyone called us, anyway." He's walking awfully slow—so slow, I can't ride my bike. I have to steer it beside me, guide it along like a blind dog. So I know he's gearing up for a pretty long tale. "Of course, *we* didn't feel like we were trouble back then. Felt like we were out finding freedom.

"We were barely older than you are now," he goes on, "hanging out one day, early on in the fall. That time of the year when it still feels good to be in a T-shirt, and all you want to do is be outside."

I smile, because Chuck has a way of telling stories that makes me feel like I'm there.

"So we were hanging out behind the church—our

41

very own Hopewell. You know how that church butts up against a big wooded lot?"

I nod. "Yeah," I say. "And the old creek where they used to do the baptisms."

"Well, we figured nobody'd come looking for us there, and it was so beautiful, full of fall colors. I remember, it was the kind of day you want to put in a bottle. Which was why we'd ditched school. We didn't think we could be in school on such a perfect fall day. And out behind the church, we were soaking it all in—the autumn sun and the leaves. And we were hiding from the truant officer. And—now, don't tell Gus, because he'd kill me for admitting this . . ." He leans down to whisper, "We were sneaking cigarettes."

"Chuck," I say.

"Shhh. Now, like I said, the sun felt really good to us that day. Must've felt good to that snake, too, because here he comes right out of the shade. Here he comes, heading straight for the light.

"Bad part was, he had to get past us so that he could stretch out on the church's nice, sun-warmed back step.

"That snake, he saw us, but he refused to skitter away. He acted like he was used to everyone being afraid of his angry-looking orange-brown stripes. He must have learned to expect it. Everybody who lives

in this part of the country knows a copperhead when they see one."

"They're unmistakable," I jump in, because my heart is racing. "Everybody knows a copperhead is poisonous."

"I saw those copper-colored stripes," Chuck says, "and I was ready to run. But your mom? She reached out and grabbed that copperhead behind his head. Grabbed him, like there was no way that snake would ever hurt her.

"Auggie, your mom stared that snake down. Stared, even while I was yelling at her to leave him alone. But she never budged. Stood there, like she was telling that snake something just by looking. And you know, when she finally put him back down, he slithered off as fast as his scaly belly would take him. Ran away, like he was scared of your mom. Probably was, too," he adds with a chuckle.

"I don't think I've ever felt quite as safe as I did right then," Chuck admits. "With your mom at my side, I knew whatever bad thing might come my way, it would take one look at her and run off, too."

My head buzzes like the beetle traps in Harold's yard as I try to figure out why Chuck told me this story. There's a reason for everything with Chuck, though. I try to take as many notes as I can, in my head, because I'm already betting that I'll need to remember his story later.

As we get closer to Serendipity Place, he says, "Let's turn down Joy Boulevard. Take the long way to your house." Chuck glances around while he walks, breathing deep like he's in the midst of something wonderful.

"Always did love this neighborhood," he says. "You know, these houses were built before electricity," he adds, as though this is really something to admire. "Wires had to be put in later on."

Not that it really matters. It's not like anybody in our neighborhood has a computer or even cable TV. We're more like taped-together rabbit-ear antennas and antique everything. As we get closer to my house, at the corner of Sunshine and Lucky, it feels like we all have as much need for electricity as a camping tent.

"Lot of history in this neighborhood," Chuck insists.

Sure. History. As I stare at my own house, I think that "history" is cloth awnings over side windows, each of them dotted with giant mismatched patches of material. It's duct tape on screen doors. It's a white-washed house with gray shutters, every inch of paint peeling like skin after a sunburn. It's a fence made out of wrought iron so rusty, nasty orange grit comes off on my hand when I touch it.

For the first time, it hits me that maybe the only fancy thing about my neighborhood is its pretty name.

"See you tomorrow," Chuck says, swinging open my front gate. "At Montgomery."

"Montgomery?" I ask. My heart beats a little faster.

"Sure. We had to find a place to hold church services," he says, his face turning as dark as a storm cloud.

"Isn't Hopewell getting fixed up?" I ask, feeling a tight, worried twist in my stomach.

"Of course," he says. "But we need a place to have church in the meantime.

"I saved everything," he goes on. "Even the tiny little broken bits from the stained-glass windows. Not sure what I'll actually do with them, but—sometimes, when you love something, the letting-go can't happen with a single sweep of the broom."

He forces a little strip of sunlight into his smile as he motions for me to walk through the open gate.

"Tomorrow then," he says.

And because I don't know how to say anything to him about the forced sunlight in his smile, I nod and agree, "Tomorrow."

· · · **10** · · ·

When I step inside Montgomery the next morning, the first thing that hits me is how scooped-out the building feels. Without the benches and the desks and the plaques and the teachers, Montgomery feels like an ice-cream cone with the Butter Brickle already licked out.

Gus steers me into the all-purpose room, though, and I instantly start to feel different. Because Chuck has set up rows of folding chairs and his own makeshift pulpit, and everyone from Serendipity Place is pretty much here already, milling around the aisles and talking and taking it all in, this new but familiar place where we'll be holding church every week. I start to feel a smile on my face—a real, honest smile.

It's good to be back at Montgomery, I think. So good, in fact, that as I look at the faces of my neighbors fill-

ing up the school I loved so much, I get a warm glow in my chest.

Old Widow Hollis—it's all we've ever called her, since she's so knobby and wrinkled, the only word we ever think of to describe her is *old*—eases herself into a folding chair and slowly stretches her feet out in front of her. She crosses her legs at the ankle, and scratches at her scalp, her frizzy white hair making her look like a dandelion gone to seed.

Widow Hollis's little great-grandson, Noah, mimics the sound of a track gun firing, sprints, and launches himself over her legs like they're hurdles.

Mrs. Shoemacker, the neighborhood ears, steps in, folding her arms over her cardigan. Without so much as a nod hello to anyone, she slinks into a seat in the back. As usual, she leans forward and listens in on everybody else, watching out the corner of her eye as the Widow Hollis grabs Noah by the back of his shirt and wraps him into her arms, saying, "Honey, every time you start acting up, I'm gonna kiss you and hug you. . . ."

Noah's face turns bright red and he struggles to free himself, eyeing me in a way that pleads with me to keep quiet about him being kissed by his grandmother in public. Noah lives with his great-grandmother, and it seems like I'm always watching the Widow Hollis use her kisses to try to embarrass him into behaving. But at six years old, Noah is a scabbed knee waiting to happen. The kind of kid who could accidentally stab himself with a pencil, spit on the bleeding hole in his hand, and move on without a second thought.

I'm still glancing around the room, taking in the sight of the members of my church packed inside of my favorite school when I hear a familiar, "Hi, Auggie," from somewhere over my shoulder.

"Lexie!" I shout. I turn and lean in to hug her, thinking, *Everything's coming back. First Montgomery, now my best friend.* But there's something funny about the way she hugs me—it's like trying to hug somebody through a mattress.

When I finally pull away, half of Lexie is missing. "You changed your hair," I say when I realize her long curls have been clipped into short spikes. "But—but why—?"

I can't believe it. Cut the way it is now, Lexie can't wear her hair any way but one. I try to put on a white lie of a smile—because I don't want to hurt her feelings. But I must have shock and disappointment smeared all over my face, because Lexie's smile gets awfully droopy, suddenly.

"I think it's cute," Victoria says as she tosses her

own perfectly combed, silky hair over her shoulder.

Lexie turns toward Victoria, trying to put her wide smile back on. But it kind of looks like a vase that's been broken and glued back together—wobbly, crooked, and about to fall apart all over again.

"Mom and I took her to my hairdresser yesterday," Victoria says, looking at Lexie's spikes admiringly.

"*That's* where you went?" I say. *To get rid of her shine?* I think, my own mouth drooping.

"Don't you love it?" Victoria asks.

I stare at Lexie, feeling sad because her hair makes her look prickly and dangerous and not like herself at all.

My stomach is a teeter-totter as I finally turn toward Victoria and ask, "What are you doing here? You don't— go to Hopewell—"

"Hey, Auggie!" Mr. Bradshaw shouts, interrupting us as he walks up to my side. "Harold and I just passed by your mom's old billboard, and it made me start thinking of her all over again."

Weird Harold walks beside his dad, his hair extra-crazy from their bicycle ride. He's carrying a jean jacket that could completely swallow him in one gulp. Probably, I figure, it's his dad's coat. Smart Harold Bradshaw is always trying to take care of his dad, making him take cod-liver oil to ward off colds in the winter, that sort of thing. This morning, he stares in a disapproving way at his dad's old rope sandals, at the feet that shouldn't be bare, not now, not in the cooler fall weather.

Victoria eyes Mr. Bradshaw, then me, and shares a look with Lexie. The look itself is like a secret passed between them.

"See you, Auggie," Victoria says, turning. I'm not sure if she means, *Nice to see you*, or *See you later*, but the way she says my name—it rings through the air in such an awful way. It sounds like the noises the sea lions at the zoo make when they bark for their dinner.

I'm still trying to remember how to make my mouth work as Ms. Dillbeck ambles in. She's kind of like a walking eggplant—same color, same shape. She leans against me a little, so that I have to start moving forward, help her toward a seat. Irma Jean follows, and I wind up getting smooshed into a chair of my own, surrounded by a few Pikes, Gus, and Ms. Dillbeck.

I glance about, wondering what happened to Lexie. I feel like my whole body's been scrubbed with a stiff wire brush when I realize she's across the room, beside Victoria.

I don't hear a single full sentence of Chuck's sermon. Mostly, I'm staring at the back of Lexie's spiky hair and Victoria's silky straight mane. The longer I stare, the more Victoria starts to look like a storm cloud, filled with winds strong enough to knock a friendship down.

At the end of the sermon, right when I'm expecting everyone to stand, Chuck points to the man sitting next to Victoria and announces, "Mr. Cole has asked if he could have a moment of your time."

Chuck steps aside, and lets Victoria's dad stand in front of us all. He's wearing a suit, but he looks comfortable in it, like maybe he's the kind of guy who wears suits all the time—even to the Fill 'N Sip for a bag of ice.

"As some of you are probably aware," Mr. Cole begins, "Reverend Taylor has already begun the task of seeking funds to renovate the Hopewell Community Church. In appealing for funds, he and I came into contact with each other. I'm on the city council, after all. As an extension of the city council—and as a result of the recent

51

storm—I've helped form a new committee. The House Beautification Committee. And that's why I came to introduce myself today."

I glance at Weird Harold. I can practically feel him bristle on the other side of the all-purpose room. He crosses his arms over his chest, and shakes his head beneath a ball cap that says I'M NOT WHO YOU THINK I AM. He's suspicious. Already.

"Following our recent storm, the House Beautification Committee would like to make sure that the sections of Willow Grove that were hit the hardest are rebuilt in a way that preserves the charm of our city. We want Willow Grove to continue to be the beautiful city it's always been.

"My daughter, Victoria, a junior member of the committee, has a few handouts," Mr. Cole goes on. Chair legs squeak as Victoria jumps to her feet, as though she's been waiting all morning for this very moment. "We simply want to remind everyone of some of the existing ordinances of Willow Grove as we all rebuild those structures hit by the storm," Mr. Cole says, grinning at us as Victoria passes out the papers like a teacher's pet.

My heart is as scraped and hot as a rug burn as she heads toward the section where I'm sitting. I try to seem completely unfazed when she hands me a printed sheet. But the truth is, I can barely even read the handout through my tears:

ATTENTION
RESIDENTS OF SERENDIPITY PLACE

A Neighborhood in Willow Grove, Missouri

A property is in violation of city codes if:

1. Any structure present on the property (including, but not limited to, a house or outbuilding) is not being adequately maintained or is deemed to be a fire hazard.

2. Any land within property boundaries (including, but not limited to, lawns, gardens, or undeveloped lots) is shown to have a significant overgrowth of brush or weeds, or grass measuring more than ten (10) inches.

3. Any land within property boundaries contains items or materials deemed to be a threat to public safety.

4. Any structure or land within property boundaries is found to be in violation of city health codes.

The owner of an offending property will receive one (1) warning notice, and a forty-five (45) day conditional grace period, during which the owner will be required to improve the condition(s) of their property.

If a property owner fails to comply, the grace period will be deemed null and void; said owner shall be fined $10–$100 a day for each of the prior forty-five (45) days and every day that it remains in violation thereafter.

The amount of the fine will be based on the severity of the offense(s).

Thank you,

The House Beautification Committee
(Making our city beautiful, one house at a time.)

"But Serendipity Place didn't get hit by the storm," Weird Harold shouts, even as his dad tries to shush him. "Not like our church did. Our neighborhood looks exactly like it did before. And what's this about yards being over- grown? What does that have to do with storm damage?"

"You're worried the committee will make you clean up your room," Irma Jean teases.

  54

Laughter spreads, loud enough to cover anything else Weird Harold tries to say. Chairs screech, too, as everyone stands and starts to leave, off to a Sunday brunch and the ambrosia salad or the fried chicken leg they've started to daydream about.

I finally get up, start saying my good-byes and helping Ms. Dillbeck out of her chair. I catch sight of Victoria— even though I don't see Lexie, I can see the red spikes of her hair sticking up above Victoria's head, the way a shark fin sticks up out of the ocean. Lexie and Victoria are walking side by side toward the exit. I decide, right then, to only miss three things about Lexie:

1. Her long red hair that she could twist into a million never-before-seen hairdos.

2. The way our laughter used to sound like it needed each other, the way piano notes need each other to form a chord.

3. The way she liked to wish with me as we stared up at my mom, the brightest star in the sky.

··· 12 ···

"Dear Mom," I scribble in my notebook, then tighten up my face as I wait for the words to start flowing. I think if I were to tell her some of what's happening—with Lexie or the church or school—it might be different, somehow. Maybe she'd show up, and I'd find out that a mother's shoulder feels different than a grampa's. That it's softer and stronger all at once.

But I'm not quite sure how to cram all this into a letter, so I put my notebook down, and set up the TV trays in the living room: one in front of Gus's chair and one in front of mine. We play tug-of-war over what we watch during dinner. When I win, we watch game shows. When Gus wins, we watch the news.

As I lay our silverware out, the station's already tuned in with the help of our duct-taped rabbit ears. The news. I wrinkle my nose, disappointed, until halfway through my corn bread and beans, when Chuck's face fills the jerky screen.

"Our church family will be having a huge rummage sale," Chuck says. "The money from the sale will be

put toward rebuilding Hopewell. We're taking donations for the sale, which can be dropped off at any
time in a bin I've set up in the parking lot of the old
Montgomery Elementary School. As the church pastor, I'm also seeking donations on a larger scale—from
construction companies and the like—anyone willing
to provide building materials, or their time. This is
going to be an enormous project. Our recent storm hit
Hopewell harder than any other building in Willow
Grove, and it's going to take time to secure funds for
a renovation. But I'm confident we'll meet our goals,
with a generous community like ours."

He smiles at the camera, and even though I can feel
Gus brightening beside me, I accidentally let out a low,
wordless grumble.

"What's that all about, Little Sister?" he asks.

"Things don't get fixed," I say. "When something's
broken, it's broken."

"Everything that gets broken can be fixed," Gus tries
to assure me.

"With what?" I snap. "Glue? Tape? With some stupid
mismatched patch?"

I hadn't meant to let my sourness leak out, but now
that I have, I can't hold any of it back, not anymore.
"It's like—" I go on, "like when something's *old.*" Finally,

I say the word like I've been feeling it the past few days. Like it's a scaly, nasty patch of dead skin. "When something's old, it's never new again."

"Nothing wrong with a thing being a little old," he says.

I grimace.

"Poor folks have poor ways, Little Sister," he insists, using the same words that I've heard hundreds of times, but have never really thought about until now. "Folks around here," he goes on, "they might not have a lot of money, but they've got pride. Everybody keeps their houses tidy. There's not one linoleum floor in this entire neighborhood that I'd have to think twice about eating off of."

That much is true. Every single day, somebody's mom is outside beating rugs or hanging sheets or scrubbing windows, big streams of white soap running down her arms. But I don't want to admit he's right. I shake my head hard enough to make my braids ripple like tall grass in the breeze.

"Little Sister," he starts.

"Why do you call me that?" I blurt. "I'm not your little sister. I'm nobody's little sister."

He leans back in his chair, eyes me suspiciously. "I call you that," he says softly, "because you're mine, every bit as much as your mom was. Child number two. A little sister."

I feel even worse than before, because now I've hurt Gus. I think I can hear his heart cracking inside his chest.

"Where's all this coming from?" he asks.

"It came from the fact that they shut down Montgomery and sent me to Dickerson," I say. "It came from the fact that Victoria Cole's in my class, and she's on the House Beautification Committee with her dad. And she—" But I can't finish: *She's got Lexie.* The sting is too fresh.

I steer around that to go on, ". . . and her hair is straight and she's like a magazine picture, and we live in a neighborhood that's—*old.*" I don't say anything about wishing Old Glory would stop picking me up in the afternoon with a wrecked car attached to her back, or how I think it's a little embarrassing now that he's a trash hauler. I've hurt him enough already.

"Well," Gus says. "Maybe we could do our own renovations."

A tiny ray of hope appears inside me, the same way a little stream of light pours from the hallway through my bedroom door's keyhole at night.

Gus must see that burst of light right away, because

he instantly warns, "Remember, we're not the kind of people who can go hire some ritzy interior decorator."

"I don't care so much about the inside," I say. "I care more about what's on the outside."

Sure, Gus and my teachers and Chuck like to talk about how the outside of a person doesn't matter as much as the inside. But all Victoria's passed judgment on are my outsides—my clothes, my grampa, Old Glory. If I ever want her to think of me differently, the *outside* is what I've got to fix.

"Think about it, Gus," I say. "Somebody who doesn't know us, who's just passing by, they look at the front of our house, and maybe they think we're run-down people. If anybody's inside our house—well, then, they know us. They know we're not run-down."

Gus smiles and nods in agreement before he offers me a big helping of his hearty pumpkin pie laugh.

··· **13** ···

I'm way too old for my wagon. Too old to be heading down the sidewalk dragging the red Radio Flyer Gus gave me back when I was about four.

But I don't care. I can't waste time feeling a little

silly, not when I'm on a mission. I'm in such a rush, I forget about keeping a safe distance between myself and the wagon, and yelp a couple of times when it nips at my heels.

I look for Chuck first at Hopewell, but the building is boarded up and deserted. The broken fragments of wood and plaster and glass the storm tore off have been swept away from the lot and the sidewalk. But the church still stands like a broken twig.

I head straight for Montgomery and find Chuck in the parking lot. He looks like half a person, the way he's bent over the lip of the donation bin, sifting through the contents. He looks like the legs-only part of a man, still wearing his black-and-white high-tops.

The squeak of my wagon wheels makes Chuck pull his head from the bin. "Hey, Auggie," he says. When Chuck says my name, it doesn't sound awful at all—it sounds chewy and sweet, like saltwater taffy.

He looks at my wagon, points, and says, "That's empty."

All I can think is, *Not for long.*

••• 14 •••

"Auggie!" our forsythia bush hisses when I get close to our backyard chain-link fence. I drop the handle of my wagon and wipe the sweat from my face. It's been a long walk back from Montgomery, hauling such a full load.

But I'm starting to think maybe my load was too heavy—because now I'm hearing things.

"Auggie!" the bush shouts again.

I squeal and start to back away.

"Don't be afraid," the bush hisses. "It's me! Look!"

I tiptoe up to the bush. When I lift a branch and peer inside, I realize that Weird Harold is standing at the chain link, too, but on the opposite side, in his yard. The lenses of his glasses shimmer in between the forsythia's yellow limbs. Today, his cap says DON'T TRUST THE NEWS.

"What are you doing with your face in that bush?" I ask, but Weird Harold gives me a, "Shhhhhh," and puts his finger to his lips.

"This is the only way we can relay secret messages," he says. "I warned you. You and Gus and Irma Jean and

Chuck—everybody at Montgomery. I said it was weird that they were interested in this neighborhood, even though it looks the same as always. None of you would listen. You laughed at me. Now, it's all coming true."

"Warned us about what?"

"The House Beautification Committee. Look at what I found in our mailbox," he whispers, stretching his arm through our shared bush to show me a notice:

ATTENTION
MARTIN BRADSHAW

An Individual Residing at 778 Joy Boulevard
Willow Grove, Missouri

The property located at the above address is currently in violation of the following ordinances mandated by the city council and enforced by the House Beautification Committee:

1.) Properties shall not have more than one (1) standardized rain barrel. This rain barrel must be covered with committee-approved mosquito screen.

2.) Vegetable gardens shall be confined to backyards, to preserve the curb appeal of all adjacent properties.

As the owner of this property, Mr. Martin Bradshaw shall have forty-five (45) days to address these issues.

If the condition of the property does not improve in that time, the House Beautification Committee will enforce fines for the prior forty-five (45) days and every day this property remains in violation thereafter.

The amount of the fine will be determined by committee vote and will be based on the severity of the offense(s).

Thank you,

The House Beautification Committee
(Making our city beautiful, one house at a time.)

"What'd your dad say?" I ask.

"Shhhh," Weird Harold scolds. "He hasn't seen it yet. It'll kill him. He cans and freezes all the stuff we grow in our gardens. It's how we make it through the winter."

"I know. You guys give plenty of your vegetables to the rest of us, too. If you'd explain that—" I start, but the bush rustles again as Weird Harold tries to push another sheet of paper through the limbs.

"I'm starting a petition," he informs me. "Against the committee."

"I don't need to be part of any petition," I say. "Gus and I don't have a garden. You're the only one in the entire neighborhood who has a front-yard garden and rain barrels. Move the front-yard garden into the back-yard, where you grow the rest of your vegetables. If you really tried, I'm sure you could make it all fit. Take one of the barrels down. That's easy enough."

"It's not just about the barrels, Auggie."

I shrug. I don't see why he's so mad.

"*Think* about it," he says. "What's beautiful? What's ugly? Their rules are as clear as chocolate syrup."

I fight the urge to make little circles in the air above my ear. If this isn't cuckoo, I don't know what is. Beauty isn't exactly hard to figure out. It's not a complicated math problem—it's *beauty.* Irma Jean starts a new project with an old hand-me-down shirt filled with stains and holes, and after she's done sewing on it, she's got a pretty new skirt that doesn't have a single frayed spot or discolored patch. Once, it was used up and ugly, and now it's pretty—obviously.

"Fine. Be that way," Weird Harold snaps, angry about the frown that confusion has etched into my face. "But you'll care when they come after *you.*"

··· 15 ···

When Gus pulls up, I tuck Weird Harold's warning into the back of my mind and rush to meet Old Glory.

"What do you want to do with all this glass, Auggie?" Gus asks when I drag him to my wagon, parked under the sweet gum tree out back.

"Not any old glass, Gus," I say. "Glass from Hopewell."

Gus leans down and takes a look. Gingerly, he slides a big piece of red out and holds it to the light. The edge looks so jagged and dangerous, it makes me nervous to see it between his fingers.

"I don't really like the idea of you picking up such sharp things when I'm not around," he says.

"I didn't—Chuck did," I say.

"But broken glass?" Gus asks, his face wrinkling.

"That came from the old stained-glass windows, Gus."

"Right," Gus says, still not seeing what I'm hinting at.

"I know that glass has already been used once," I say. "But maybe we could use it, too. The same way Irma Jean sews new outfits out of fabric that's already been worn by somebody else. Maybe that glass might like to find a new home in a new window—nothing as important as Hopewell's. But a nice, cozy little window where it can get plenty of sun, just the same."

A slow smile spreads across Gus's face. "Got it!" he shouts.

Of the two windows that face the front porch, we start with the one that's the easiest to get to—the one next to the door, with nothing in its way, not even the old swing. Gus takes off the screen, so he can get closer to the wooden slats that divide the window into eight equal sections. He cuts one of those eight clear panes out, leaving a hole that looks like a spot in a mouth where somebody's wiggled a loose tooth free.

"Sure am glad it's decided to turn cold," Gus says, pointing at the missing pane. "No problems with mosquitoes today."

Gus measures the hole and cuts a new pane out of a big chunk of scarlet glass. He winks at me when he gets it set in right. "Little Sister," he says, "this is a fantastic idea. Quick—what color do you want the next pane to be?"

Gus and I become a two-man team. Gus cuts new panes out of glass—panes tinted fuchsia and purple and green and blue. I come along behind him with some old glazing putty that Gus had in the garage, which is white sticky gunk that makes sure the glass stays in place tight and solid.

"Really pack that stuff in good, Little Sister," Gus says. "We don't want a bunch of cold, drafty air leaking in on us this winter."

When we get the first window completely done, all eight panes, we rush out into the middle of the front yard to get a good look.

"It's like—it's like—" I stutter, but I can't find the right words.

"Come here," Gus says, tugging on my sleeve. When we race inside, Gus steps right in front of our new window. "Watch this," he says.

He holds both his arms out like a scarecrow. But it only takes a couple of seconds for me to stop thinking *scarecrow*. Instead, I start to think *mistletoe* and *fat holiday stockings* and *candy canes*.

Because that's exactly how Gus looks. With his arms held out, the colored light dances off the sleeves of his white shirt so that he looks like a lit-up Christmas tree.

I clap. "This is amazing, Gus!"

"Told you it was a good idea, Little Sister," Gus says. "Come on now, let's do the other window."

Together, we rush outside like it really is Christmas.

Like carolers are on the lawn and Santa is on the roof, dancing between crisp, clean snowflakes.

But even when we finish both windows, it's not enough. I glance down into my wagon, at the tiny little shards on the bottom, and say, "Too bad we can't scatter this on the ground—or down the front walk."

I've never seen Gus run to Old Glory so fast. I break into a pant to keep up with him and hop in. I'm so excited to find out where we're going that I pet the dash right along with him. "Come on, Old Glory," I chant. "You can do it. Come on."

Somehow, the whole town looks a little fresher as we drive.

We wind up at the hardware store, where Gus buys an enormous bag of QUIKRETE concrete mixture—a whole eighty pounds—for a little over three dollars.

"*This* we can fit in the budget," he announces happily.

Back home, Gus adds water to the dry mix, turning it into gray mud, and starts spreading it over our cracked front walk. I crouch down low, dragging my wagon behind me. I lay thumbnail-sized pieces of glass on the wet concrete, pushing them deep enough to cover all the sharp edges, but not so deep that the smooth tops won't be able to sparkle in the sun. Once it's dry, it'll be safe to walk on.

When we're done, we race each other to the end of the front yard.

"It's like looking straight into a kaleidoscope," I say. "The way all those brightly colored pieces shimmer in the sunlight."

Only, it's not a kaleidoscope—it's where we live.

··· 16 ···

On Monday, Ms. Byron tells us to crack open our math books. "Groups of three!" she shouts. "Hurry, hurry!" By now I'm not really all that upset about her nervousness. In fact, it doesn't seem like a bad thing at all. All that energy reminds me of a curious kitten who's always jumping and pawing at you, trying to get you to play.

I immediately push my desk toward Victoria and Lexie, slamming into them so hard that all three of our desks rattle like cymbals. I think I see Victoria and Lexie exchange an eye roll, but I brush it away like lunch crumbs caught in a skirt.

I pull out my ten-cent folder with loose-leaf paper inside and a plain old yellow number two. Victoria and Lexie pull out spiral notebooks plastered with glittery hearts and uncap matching pens with giant pink feathers poking out the back.

Lexie's bought the same school supplies as Victoria. I try to tell myself it doesn't matter, even as my breaking heart insists that it does.

"I hate fractions," Victoria moans as she clicks her pen in a rhythm: *click-click, click. Click-click, click.* Like a woodpecker.

Lexie's eyes immediately shoot toward me. She knows I love them. But it suddenly seems silly to admit that math is my favorite subject.

I already know the answers to the first four. I'm not exactly a whiz at math, but I've always been able to do fractions in my head. I imagine that I'm like Gus—I have a fiery welding torch in my hand, and I'm fusing the numbers together or cutting them apart.

Victoria starts to doodle right in the margin of her textbook. "This is impossible," she moans.

Even though I've been trying to hold it in, my news is frothing and bubbling—like foam from a two liter of Coke that's fallen from a grocery bag and bounced down the front steps. It's spewing everywhere inside me, racing up my neck toward my mouth.

"Westartedworkingonourhouse!" I blurt, so fast my words pile on top of each other.

71

Victoria glances up at me like I've torn off all my clothes.

"We—Gus and I—started working on our house," I say, slower this time.

Victoria frowns, letting her eyes trail across my plain green folder and my yellow number two, my discount-bin sweater, and my last year's jeans. She stares an extra-long time at the jeans Gus bought summer before last, big enough that I could get two winters out of them. He hemmed them, like he always does—and now that I've grown tall enough for him to take them down again, I've got little white circles around both ankles.

"How?" Victoria asks, still staring at those circles. It's as though she's asking those circles, not me. As though she's saying there's no way Gus and I could ever have the money to fix up our house.

"We've been making it beautiful—just like the committee wants," I say.

"But—how?" Victoria asks again.

"We've got stained-glass windows—and a stained-glass front walk."

"A stained-glass front walk?" Lexie repeats, rising up out of a slouch.

"It's the most amazing thing," Irma Jean insists,

swiveling in her chair to face our group. "I couldn't believe it when I stepped outside this morning and saw it."

Victoria squints at Irma Jean. It's only a squint, but right then, it seems like she's saying Irma Jean is so far beneath her, she's got to really strain her eyes to see Irma Jean clearly.

That Victoria has some nerve! I think as I tighten my lips and curl myself over my loose-leaf paper. I hate the way she can't seem to see any of the kids from Montgomery without seeing the bottom tip of her own nose, too.

Quick as a cat can flick her whiskers, I answer every problem in our math assignment, rip my paper from my folder, and toss it on top of Victoria's textbook.

"You can't do all those problems that fast," she says.

"Go ask Ms. Byron if they're right," I say. "After she tells you they are, I can explain them to you."

While Victoria stomps toward Ms. Byron's desk with my paper in her hand, I'm left alone with Lexie. As the silence between us tightens, I have to remind myself that I can only miss three things about Montgomery. Just three.

··· 17 ···

At the end of the day, everybody rolls out of the Dickerson doors. I don't think I can roll today—I stomp instead, each step rough and jerky.

On the front walk, I watch Lexie get into the Coles' car again. I want to tell Lexie that if she lived a few blocks south, in my neighborhood, Victoria would probably be looking down her nose at her, too. But Victoria's got Lexie thinking she's as perfect as a brand-new piece of jewelry behind glass. So Lexie wouldn't believe me, anyway.

When I glance up, I see Harold and Irma Jean exchanging a look. The kind of look that says they've been talking about me. "I know," I tell them. "I shouldn't have exploded at Victoria. But I couldn't help it."

I glance down, cringing at the sight of our ankles. We all have the same mark of last year's jeans. "I *hate* those white circles," I grumble.

Irma Jean flinches at my harsh tone. "What do you mean?"

"It's like we're branded," I say. "It's like a mark that

74

says the three of us are all from a poor neighborhood."

"I never really paid any attention to them before," Irma Jean confesses, leaning forward to point her head down toward her feet.

"Listen, Auggie," Weird Harold starts, using that same, overly soft tone I've heard him use on his dad when he's about to try to talk him into something. "You and I both want the same thing."

"Maybe, maybe not," I say, bristling.

"Sure we do," Harold says, smiling at me from underneath a ball cap that says BIGFOOT LIVES.

"We want the House Beautification Committee to see the beauty in our homes," Harold insists.

"I don't care about the committee as much as you do," I say, my eyes zeroed in on the black car that's carrying Victoria and Lexie away.

"But *Victoria*'s on the committee," Harold reminds me.

I glance over at him, feeling my eyes widen.

"My dad's always saying you catch more flies with honey," he says.

"Gus says that."

"So . . . maybe we shouldn't fight with Victoria," Harold suggests.

"I watched her," Irma Jean pipes up. "She got real

stiff when you stood up to her. Her whole body. Like suddenly, she became a brick wall."

"I saw it, too," Harold says. "So I was thinking— maybe Auggie shouldn't try to pick a fight. Maybe I shouldn't try to relay secret messages or start a petition. Maybe we need a better strategy. Maybe we need a little sugar."

"Like—maybe if I invite them over!" I shout. "I could ask Victoria and Lexie both to come—as long as Gus and I had enough time to really work on our house first. Then they could see all the great things we've done to the place."

He nods, smiling. "Now you're talking."

"Like an open house!" I say. "You guys would be there, right? When Victoria sees our house, she'll know—we're not run-down people." *And Lexie will remember that, too,* I tell myself.

"I could make new curtains for my own front window," Irma Jean offers.

"Dad and I could clean up the front yard," Harold chimes in.

"You said it wasn't about the rain barrels," I remind him.

"It's not—but—" Weird Harold rubs his chin. "I think we have a better chance of impressing Victoria—

and the House Beautification Committee—if we work together."

"Almost like an open *neighborhood*," Irma Jean marvels.

"What if they say no?" I wonder. "When I ask them to come over?"

"Tomorrow, at recess, we'll *all* ask them," Harold says. "They won't be able to refuse if we all insist they come. In the meantime, the three of us can start working. Okay?"

Irma Jean nods and puts her hand out, palm down. Harold piles his hand on top of hers, and I put mine on top of Harold's, just like a team would before a big game.

· · · 18 · · ·

"You really coming to work with me today?" Gus asks that afternoon, after we drop Weird Harold and Irma Jean off at their houses.

"Absolutely," I say as we wave Irma Jean good-bye, and she scurries up her front steps. "Don't want you taking something to McGunn's that we could be using for our house."

It's far warmer today than it really should be for September. But that's Missouri for you. People around here are always saying, "If you don't like the weather in Missouri, just wait five minutes and it'll change." Once, when I was still going to school at Montgomery, the morning bell rang at the start of a sunny, early spring day. Soon after, the skies clouded up, and it rained so much that we couldn't go out for morning recess. By lunch, afternoon snowflakes were bouncing off our windows. We gobbled down our sandwiches and ran to the playground for a snowball fight. By the time we went home, the snow had melted, and the sun was back out.

I swear it's true. I've got yearbook pictures to prove it.

Old Glory rumbles and jiggles toward Gus's scheduled pickup.

"Hey there, Gus," a man calls out from his front yard. He's wearing jeans and a white short-sleeved shirt that's unbuttoned to show off his undershirt. Kind of old-fashioned for men to wear undershirts like that. The only other one I know who likes them is Gus.

"Hey, Burton," Gus says, waving as he steps from the truck.

A big SOLD sign is stuck into the middle of his yard, next to a pot filled with flowers that have sharp petals, like daisies, but in the same colors as autumn leaves. Mums, I think they're called.

"Really thought I'd have more for you," Burton apologizes. He shuffles his feet, tucks his chin down toward his chest, almost as though to hide his embarrassment as he points at the cardboard boxes piled at the curb. "Don't know that you can get much of anything at McGunn's for this."

I stand over Gus as he squats and riffles through the cardboard boxes. They're full of toasters and lamp parts and hair curlers and coffeepots and irons.

"Just a bunch of stuff I swore I'd fix someday," Burton admits. "Stuff we plugged into the socket one morning, only to wind up getting showered with sparks and snaps."

Gus nods, understanding.

"Got one more box in the house," Burton says. "If you even want it."

"Sure, sure," Gus says, because he's a sweet guy. He'd never in a million years tell someone that their junk is too junky, even for a trash hauler.

As Burton disappears back into his house, I smile at Gus. "Look," I say, riffling through the box. "This toaster still gleams, even if it can't toast a piece of bread anymore."

Gus whistles as he slides the toaster from the box and holds it to the sun. "Sure does, Little Sister," he agrees. "Almost need a pair of sunglasses to look at it."

He frowns as he thinks. "There's only so much you can do with an old thing like this," he admits. "It's not like we can cut it up like the stained glass—"

Suddenly, Gus stops talking. He flashes a smile so wide and full, it swallows the rest of him right up. "Can't cut it up," Gus chuckles through that Cheshire cat grin, "unless you've got the tools to cut it with."

"Like, say, an old welding torch lying around in a shed?" Now I've got my own Cheshire grin.

Burton and his white undershirt appear again, along with the last of his promised boxes.

"You sure you want this, Gus?" Burton asks, still embarrassed.

"You bet we do," Gus says, taking the box out of Burton's arms with such care, you'd think it was filled with about fifty eggs.

"And if you find anything else in there, anything at all, even so much as a pencil that's been snapped in two, you give us a call," I add.

Gus winks at me, his dark eyes shining brighter than the side of the toaster.

··· 19 ···

The door of the shed where Gus keeps his welding tools actually lets out a gasp when we open it. Like it's been holding its breath waiting for us to arrive.

I know exactly how that old shed feels. I can barely remember to breathe as Gus lowers one of his masks over my face and puts some fireproof gloves on my hands. I feel myself fidgeting anxiously as he pulls Burton's toaster out of the box. "When you look at this," Gus says, "what can you see?"

"A flower," I say. "With big pointy petals, like a daisy. If a daisy could be silver, that is."

Gus smiles. "You got it," he says. He puts a cutting tip on his torch, flips his own welding mask down over his eyes, and motions for me to stand back. Once I take a few backward steps, he angles the torch, slices the toaster in half, removes the guts, and cuts the outline of a daisy head.

I watch for a little while, then turn back to the big cardboard box. I pull out an old curling iron. "Here, Gus," I say. "We can use this as the stem." I open the iron and point to the part that clamps hair down. "Can you bend this like a leaf?"

"You bet," Gus says. He uses his torch to remove the metal barrel from the handle. He exchanges his cutting torch for a welder that uses a flame to melt the daisy head to the stem. And he heats up the clamp on the old curling iron enough that he can bend it the way I described.

As quickly as Mrs. Pike can pull her twins apart when they start to fight, Gus and I have a whole flower—a silver daisy.

When we're done, we rush outside, where Gus holds the daisy up to the sun.

"Gus!" I shout. But I have so many thoughts swarming inside me, it's hard to pull the words apart to make sense of it all.

I grab some loose-leaf paper from my backpack and some old crayons from my room. I sit down on our front step and start to draw the wild pictures that are exploding in my mind like popcorn kernels.

I draw a giant rose that hasn't completely opened. The petals are all swirly and tight, like a family hugging each other at the bus station, crying because none of them want to let go. On the stem, I draw giant thorns so big, they look like nails. I draw a tulip, too, as bright as the ones that grew along our curb last spring. And I draw a forget-me-not with only one petal left—the one that says *He loves me.*

"Can we make all of these, Gus?" I ask, handing him the drawings. "And—and can we make an iris, like at the Widow Hollis's place? And grass—like the kind in Mrs. Shoemacker's yard? Grass as thick as the carpet in movie stars' houses!"

Gus's Cheshire cat grin comes back. "Sure, Little Sister," he says. The sweat of work makes him glisten like a tub full of pennies.

··· 20 ···

"Lexie," I call during our morning recess the next day. I can tell, from the way her walk hesitates, that she's heard her name. I can tell, too, from the way that she links her arm with Victoria's and quickens her pace, that she's ignoring me.

The way that she's racing to get away from me rips me apart, like I'm being attacked by a vicious dog.

"Lexie," I repeat, louder this time, rushing to catch up to her. Harold and Irma Jean are with me, working so hard to keep up, the toes of their sneakers take a couple of bites out of my heels.

We're running so fast that the Halloween decorations on Dickerson's classroom windows fly past like the pages in an old flip book. *"Lexie!"* I shout so loud that everyone at the swing set and the teeter-totters turn toward me.

Their stares finally get her to turn around. "What?" she hisses. She eyes Victoria and shrugs, as if to tell her that she certainly hasn't done anything to encourage me to keep following after her.

"I-" I stutter, trying to remember what I was going to say. "I . . ." But my words get stuck in the back of my throat as I stare into her face, which looks upset and maybe even a little irritated. This is a face you turn toward a pesky little brother, not a face for a best friend.

How is it that I'm nervous trying to get Lexie's attention? How is it that I annoy her so much—or is it that I embarrass her? Does the fact that we were friends embarrass her now? The way her eyes dart back and forth makes me think she doesn't want anyone to pay much attention to the fact that we're talking.

"I wanted to invite you over. Both of you," I say, trying to make my voice sound as smooth as river rock, and not nervous at all.

"I don't think—" Lexie starts, but I don't let her get the whole answer out.

"To see our house," I insist. "Gus and I are working

on it, you know. And Irma Jean is putting up new curtains in her front window, and Harold and his dad are working on their front yard."

Lexie is still shaking her head. It hits me that she's so wrapped up in Victoria that she wants to agree with her on everything. So if I can convince *Victoria* to come over, Lexie will change her mind, too.

"Bring your camera," I tell Victoria. "As a junior member of the House Beautification Committee, you could take photos of our improvements, and bring them back for the other members to see. I bet they'd all really appreciate that."

This sort of swells Victoria up, like she's a puffer fish ready to explode.

"Nice," Weird Harold hisses in my ear. "Great strategy."

"We should go," Victoria tells Lexie. "When?" she asks, looking at me.

"A week from Friday," I say.

When Lexie nods an *okay,* I see some sort of flicker in her eyes. She looks like she's about to tell me something—maybe even a secret, judging by the way she starts to lean in.

Instead, Victoria grabs Lexie's arm and starts to haul her away as she announces, with a voice as forceful as a swift kick, "We'll be there."

"Dear Mom," I write later that day, sitting cross-legged on the front walk of Dickerson. "I know you remember the house where Gus and I live. Gus still has the notches in the kitchen where he used his pocketknife to cut into the wall, to show how much you grew. The notches aren't real sharp anymore, especially the ones at the bottom, because I like to run my fingers over where you used to stand. I smoothed them out pretty good.

"Other things have changed, not on the inside, but the outside. I bet if you'd come back and see it, you'd be so happy, your cheeks would ache from smiling.

"I'm having an open house a week from Friday, and I wish you'd be there." It's the first time I've ever asked Mom straight-out to come home.

I'm still staring down at my words, daydreaming about the pride that will wash over Mom's face as she pulls to a stop in front of our house, when Old Glory starts honking like crazy. I know it's her—I can recognize Old Glory's voice as easily as I recognize Gus's. I fold my letter up in thirds real quick and slip it into my jacket pocket.

As Irma Jean and Harold climb into the cab, I realize that Gus has filled the bed of Old Glory with cans of paint. There must be fifty of them back there, all in different shades: lavender and sage and pumpkin and lemon and scarlet and navy and dinosaur green, and that's only for starters. As many colors as there are in a crayon box, it looks like—maybe more.

"Where'd you get all that?" I ask.

"From the hazardous waste disposal," Gus says. "Can you believe they were free?"

"Hazardous waste?" I say through a crinkle in my face. "Isn't that for dangerous stuff? Toxic stuff?"

"You can't throw away wet paint," Gus says. "So when construction companies wind up with too much of a certain color, they drop it off at hazardous waste. The cans are ours for the taking!"

"What do you think you'll do with it?" Irma Jean asks.

"The shutters," I say, getting so excited, my insides burn. "We can paint each shutter a different color—the same way the panes in the windows are all different colors! Oooh—and maybe the railing—and the porch swing—and the front door—the garage door—the mailbox!"

87

Gus laughs. "Now, now," he says. "We'll have to see how much paint we really have in all those cans first."

We drive home as quick as Old Glory can manage. We drop off Weird Harold, who's anxious to get started on his own projects.

Irma Jean needs some sort of supply from Gus before she can race up her own front steps. I can't quite imagine what Gus could have that would help her with curtains, but while I wait for him to come back, I climb into Old Glory's bed so I can get a better look at all our paint.

I'm picking up cans to read the names of the colors when I hear the rustle from the pocket of my jean jacket—the letter I just wrote to Mom.

"Hey, Gus," I say, after Irma Jean goes home and he comes back out of the garage, carrying brushes and a tarp. I lean over the side of Old Glory's bed to hand him my letter.

He darkens right up when he realizes what I've given him.

In not sure why, though. I've been writing to Mom ever since I could hold a pencil. Since Mom sends presents for Christmas and my birthday every year, Gus must know her address. I figure even if *I've* never seen a return address on any of my presents, it had to have been on the boxes somewhere in order for them to get to me. So every time I write a new letter, I give it to Gus, and he says he'll take care of it. I've never gotten an answer from Mom, but I've never quit trying, either.

Every once in a while, I even send her a gift. Nothing fancy—mostly school pictures or something little, like a hankie with her initial or a pretty pocket mirror I bought with my allowance. Just something to let her know I've been thinking about her.

"I thought you weren't doing that anymore," he says quietly.

"Writing to Mom?" I say. "Of course I am. What would she think when she keeps sending me presents, and I don't write to her at all?"

He shakes his head. "It's just been a while since you've given me one of your letters. That's all," he says, sliding it out of my hand. "I'll be sure to send it for you."

· · · 22 · · ·

A couple of days later, I'm standing in the middle of the street eyeballing our work when Ms. Dillbeck pops out of nowhere to block the sun with her eggplant body.

89

"I had to come get a closer look," Ms. Dillbeck says. "You and Gus sure have been working up a storm."

I nod, staring at the shutters that are all a different color and the rainbow that swirls around the porch railing. "I'm not exactly the best artist in the world," I tell her. "In art class, colored pencils and paintbrushes always feel about as natural to me as chopsticks. But I figured I could paint up the front of my house. *That* shouldn't really take any special talent. Still," I say as I look up into Ms. Dillbeck's face, "something's missing."

Behind Ms. Dillbeck's shoulder, the venetian blinds are parted in Mrs. Shoemacker's house. Mrs. Shoemacker's fingers hold the slats open, and her face is pressed into the space between them. When she realizes I'm looking right at her, she lets go of the blinds in a quick snap that makes me flinch.

"I really like your flower boxes," Ms. Dillbeck says, drawing my attention away from Mrs. Shoemacker's house as she points to the metal iris and marigolds and long strands of grass that Gus and I made from all the objects in Burton's boxes.

I shake my head. "I'm having people over soon, and the house needs to be—*more*." My stomach falls down between my knees as I stare. "I wanted to fix the place

90

up," I admit, "but I also wanted the house to say something. About me and Gus."

"Like what?"

I sigh. "First, it was that I wanted to show we're not shabby. Now, though—'not shabby' doesn't seem right. I mean, me and Gus—we're a lot more than that. Right?"

"So you don't just want to patch up a few rotten spots in boards," Ms. Dillbeck says. "You want to talk with your renovations. Tell a story."

I nod, eagerly, because somehow, Ms. Dillbeck seems to know exactly what's in my heart. "A story about who Gus and I are," I say, spilling over with excitement. Talking about it makes it all clear: *I want the outside of the house to say something about who we are.*

"Get your wagon," Ms. Dillbeck announces. "I've got something for you."

Okay, so I've lived in Serendipity Place my entire life. But it's not like I've spent a hundred hours inside every one of these houses. If somebody blindfolded me, shoved me into Ms. Dillbeck's living room, and yanked the blindfold off, I'd have no idea where I was standing. So I don't know what to expect as I grab the handle of my wagon and follow after her.

When I step inside her front hall, I'm surrounded by drawings, every single one of them framed.

"You must have a lot of kids," I say, pointing at the pictures.

"My nephew sent those," Ms. Dillbeck says.

"He must draw an awful lot," I say. "What grade is he in?"

"He's grown now."

"And he still draws like that?" I ask. Because the pictures on her wall don't look like anything an adult has done. They look more like something that came out of a kindergarten art class.

Ms. Dillbeck laughs softly. "He sent them. He didn't draw them."

Now I'm really confused. I want to ask why her nephew would have taken all that time to send her those pictures he didn't even draw—and why she would frame them. Frames, I figure, are for really special things.

But before I can say anything, she leads me into her old sunroom. The autumn sun streams into the room in beams that crisscross through the screen. Sort of looks like the sunlight's been cross-stitched here.

The insides of an old cardboard box rattle and clink as Ms. Dillbeck slides it out from under a table. When it gets close enough for me to look inside, I see a bunch of old broken pottery—cups and vases, their smooth glazes sparkling in the cross-stitched sunlight.

"This your nephew's, too?" I ask.

She nods. "He tried his hand at pottery for a while, but it turned out that he was better at buying art than making it."

She lifts a strange mug that's caved in on one side. She turns it over in her hand, eyeing the clumps of hardened clay that rise and fall around the lip like the mountains in the relief maps at school.

"Look at this silly old cup," she tells me. "I always loved it because my nephew made it. But it's not like I can drink out of it."

"You're giving me that for my house?" I ask, feeling bubbles of excitement rise inside me.

"I know you can figure out how to make this talk for you," she says with a wink, just before she puts the mug back and helps me hoist the box of pottery into my wagon.

· · · 23 · · ·

"The posts, Gus," I say, pointing at the simple, square poles that stretch from the floor of our porch to hold up our roof. "We could use Ms. Dillbeck's pottery to fix up the old posts, like we used the glass on the front walk."

Gus takes Ms. Dillbeck's pieces into the back shed, where he puts them into an old pillowcase and smacks them with a hammer—not hard enough to turn them into dust. Just enough to break the old cups and half-finished vases into chunks the size of a quarter. He mixes up some QUIKRETE—thicker than before—and I come along with the pieces of pottery, squishing them into the gloppy mixture as far up as I can reach. I haul a small step stool out of the garage and use it to reach the middle sections of the porch posts. For the highest sections, Gus plants his ladder and I pass him bits of pottery, telling him exactly where I want each piece to go.

Gus and I are in the middle of the front yard examining our work when I hear footsteps. I look up as Weird Harold joins us, wearing a cap that reads WHAT NOW?

"What do you think?" I ask, pointing. The concrete and pottery give the posts a thick, rough, almost dangerous feel—like the skin on the back of an iguana.

"Ms. Dillbeck's pottery, right?" he says, his crooked teeth flashing through his grin.

Part of me wonders how he knows about Ms. Dillbeck's pottery, while the other part is used to Weird Harold being able to see and know everything, like the cameras inside the door at Walmart.

So I nod, feeling pride start to leak out of my pores. "Think Victoria will like it?"

Instead of answering, Harold says, "I have something I want to show you."

He hurries across the yard, disappearing around the corner of my house.

The Bradshaw backyard almost looks like a farm, with all the rows of vegetables and the tiny signs marking what's growing where: turnips and pumpkins and beets and eggplant. The picnic tables have a few already picked zucchini spread out on them. I love the look all the rows of green shoots give the backyard—and the earthy smell of so many plants.

Harold points to his dad, who's tugging at a tarp that's draped over some large mound beside the back fence. The tarp makes an awful rattling noise, like a whole class of kids erupting into a coughing fit. As we walk closer, Harold's dad peels the tarp all the way back, to reveal a heap of metal that actually *looks* sick—all rusted and rotted. "For you," his dad says. "Our Monte Carlo."

"But what if you ever need it?" I blurt. No one's ever given me something so big before—a gift I could literally get crushed beneath. "You might not be able to ride your bike sometime—"

"I can't drive it anymore," Mr. Bradshaw admits. "It's been parked out here so long, the tires have rotted. The fluids inside have turned to acid and started to eat through the hoses. It's rusted pretty bad. Turns out there's only so much a few tarps can do to protect a car."

"We might have been able to sell it," Harold admits quietly, "if we'd put it on blocks in a garage like we should have. But now, it's not worth anything."

"When I first parked this car out here, I wasn't really sure how much I'd wind up using my bike," Mr. Bradshaw explains. "I parked it and started using the bike to save money on gas. Figured that I could keep this old car just in case, but—it's been so long since I've driven it, it's fallen apart. I'd started to think the thing was completely useless. Until you started working on your house."

"For the house," I repeat, shocked.

Mr. Bradshaw shakes his head sadly as he stares at his car. "I wish I could make the thing move again," he admits. "That's what a car is for, isn't it? Moving?"

That gives me an idea.

"Gus!" I shout, racing toward the front of my house. "Gus! Wait till you see this!"

··· 24 ···

"Nothing wants to come to an end," I tell Gus, borrowing the words he'd used to describe storms. "Not a man, not a plant, and not a car, either. A car doesn't want to get squashed. A car wants to keep moving," I insist, now borrowing Mr. Bradshaw's words. "Think of it, Gus—all those gears and wheels and spinning parts. Those beautiful, shining bumpers! Think of what we could make!"

Gus stares at me, his face a blank space on a test sheet. He's still deciding what he thinks.

"Wind chimes, Gus!" I shout. Because it would be so much fun if our house also sounded pretty.

Gus rubs the stubbly whiskers on his chin, thinking. When his face starts to disappear beneath one of those Cheshire grins, I know I've got him.

Gus and I pull the fan from the engine. He drills holes in the blades, and we hang springs and gears and nuts and bolts from long threads of wire. Together, we hang the finished wind chime from the top of the porch. The fan spins and the pieces knock against each other, making notes that sound like they've come from a xylophone. It's like the wind has grown fingers, and I've given it an instrument to play.

We make three more wind chimes. We use a hub-cap, a license plate, and the steering wheel to dangle the metal Monte Carlo symbol pried from the trunk, the door handles, the radio antenna, the hood ornament, even pieces of the grille Gus has sliced with his cut-ting torch. Together, all four chimes play a tune that reminds me of some of the songs I can hear the Widow Hollis play on her piano when she has her front win-dows open.

So much of the car is still left over. Only four days stand between us and our open house.

"More flowers—but not little flowers, this time, Gus!" I shout. "Enormous flowers! Tall as a man!" Be-cause if the rest of the car isn't going to move anymore, at least it will stand tall and proud. Besides, the metal flowers we already have are so small, it's a little hard to see their details from the street.

Gus fires up his torch again. I'm holding up metal pieces, saying, "Why don't we use this bumper as a stem?" or, "These window cranks could be the thorns on a rose!" or, "Couldn't we cut these two hubcaps to look like unopened buds?"

I start to wonder how you know for sure if something really *is* your shine. When did Irma Jean officially know she was a good seamstress? When did Lexie realize she could come up with all those wild hairdos? Did they ever trip up and have to start a new skirt or a braid over again—or does a shine always come easily?

I don't have enough time to think too much about it, not with all these new ideas popping up everywhere I look.

"Headlights," I tell Gus. "The headlights can be the centers of giant sunflowers!"

His grin is so bright I can almost see it glowing behind his welding mask.

For the next few days, we work on a whole slew of flowers, modeling most of them after the pictures in a book I've checked out from the library: orchids with their big fleshy petals. Gladiolas with three or four blossoms on the same stem. Carnations with folds and folds of petals inside. Blooms of baby's breath as big as Gus's head. We even make a few mums—just like the ones I saw out at Burton's house.

When we're finished with the flowers, the smallest ones come all the way up to my chin. Most are as tall—or taller, even—than Gus. But they're heavy and they keep falling over every time we try to "plant" them.

Gus tugs on his bottom lip, thinking. "We need to find something solid that we could tie them to."

My eyes scan our house. They stop when they hit the chimney.

The neighbors cluster across the street—some of them with binoculars pressed up against their eyes—as Gus helps me off the ladder and onto the roof.

"They're worried about you," he says. "*I'm* worried about you."

"Oh, Gus," I say. "I'm not going to fall. Promise."

I whistle to myself, until Gus finally follows my lead, adding harmony to my tune.

"Pass me that hammer, there, Auggie."

"You got it," I say, reaching for the tool with one hand while holding an enormous pansy up with the other. The way I have to bend myself around, it's like I'm playing a game of Twister up there on the roof.

We hammer nails through the holes Gus has drilled into the bottoms of the metal flowers, then use bright red rope to attach the flowers to the chimney. We tie the rope in a gigantic bow, so that it looks like a red ribbon holding a bouquet of flowers together.

It reminds me of the fancy bouquets inside the door of the Super Saver grocery. The bouquets Gus and I can never afford because we're always needing more boring stuff like bread and milk and flour. Now, we've got the biggest, brightest bouquet of all!

With the xylophone clank of wind chimes filling the air, and a bouquet on the roof, and the rainbow of colors swirling across the front of our home, I feel like we're officially ready for tomorrow's open house.

· · · 25 · · ·

Friday is sheer torture. I swear there's a lasso on the minute hand on the clock in Ms. Byron's class, and it's holding time back, keeping it from passing like it should. The time between the first bell and lunch lasts longer than my whole summer break did. The afternoon feels even longer.

When the final bell does ring, I feel a little stuck in my desk, for a minute. Like I can't quite believe the time for the open house is finally here. When Victoria pauses at my desk, looks down at me and asks, "We're still on for this afternoon, right?" I finally jump to my feet and nod. My heart burns hotter than a chunk of charcoal in a barbecue.

Old Glory scoops up Lexie and Harold and me from the Dickerson parking lot. But nobody's really talking much. We drop off Weird Harold, who smiles back at us nervously before heading through his door. Gus has just pulled Old Glory into our drive when Irma Jean tells me, "Don't go inside yet, Auggie. I have something for you."

Irma Jean sprints for her house while I lean against Old Glory, giving my weight to her front fender. I'm trying to ignore the way my blood flows through my body with the force of storm rains when I catch my reflection in her chrome bumper. I work on my face, trying to figure out how not to look worried or afraid.

I jump when Irma Jean's front door bangs open. "Auggie!" Irma Jean shouts as she comes running toward me with a pair of jeans folded up in her arms. When she hands them to me, I recognize the wear on the waistband and the small chocolate stain on the front pocket.

"These are mine," I say. "Where'd you get—" I hold them by the waistband as the legs tumble down. And I realize that Irma Jean has embroidered the ankles. Both of them. Right over the white circles.

"I asked Gus for a pair of your jeans the day we decided to have an open neighborhood," Irma Jean confesses. "So that when Lexie and Victoria come over, we won't be branded. That's what you said, right? That the circles branded us?"

I could cry looking at what Irma Jean's done. "But you—"

"I did a pair for me," Irma Jean says. "Harold says he wants to wear the same khakis he usually saves for church."

I give Irma Jean a hug and race inside. I tear through my closet, until I find a shirt that goes with the embroidery on my jeans—a deep, rusty red that also matches the nervous feeling in my chest.

Once I'm dressed, I pace the living room so quickly, I figure I could wear a hole straight through the floor before anybody shows up.

Finally, Irma Jean appears in her own embroidered jeans, with a new blouse she's made out of one of Anna Beth's dresses. And Weird Harold comes over with his hair gelled across the top of his head. He's left his baseball hats with all his wild messages at home. He doesn't even do that when we go to church.

"Refreshments!" Gus shouts, carrying a fresh pitcher of sweet tea and caramel apples, perfect for fall.

I can tell by the look on his face that he wants just as badly as the rest of us for the committee to be impressed by all our hard work. In the quiet that falls through our living room, the squeak of the front gate blares through our front window like a trumpet.

"They're here!" Irma Jean hisses, and we all race for the door at once.

Lexie and Victoria have dropped their bicycles on the sidewalk in front of our gate. They're both still wearing the same clothes they had on at school, like this isn't really all that special to them. Not like it is to us.

My eyes scan the street as I look for a car that's out of place, new. Something that Mom might be driving up in. There's no sign of her—not yet, anyway. But there's still time.

"Hello, Mr. Jones," Victoria says, nodding at Gus.

"Gus, please," he says, holding the tray of apples out to Victoria.

"No, thank you," she says. Even though her words are polite, they still feel sharp and cold.

She pulls a camera out of her backpack, and it makes a funny electronic sound when she turns it on. She starts taking pictures at the same time that Lexie wanders up the front walk.

Lexie's eyes fly open wide as she takes in the wind chimes and the paint and the glitter at her toes. "I can't believe this place!" she shouts, smiling at me as she climbs up onto the step. "It's incredible!"

Right then, Lexie kind of reminds me of a long-lost pet that's found its way home. Here she is, coming

back like she's never been away—she plops down in the exact same spot that was always hers, the second step from the top, on the right, next to the railing. When Gus offers her an apple, she instantly takes one off of the tray and starts crunching.

I could jump with happiness.

"Aren't the colors on Auggie's house beautiful?" Harold asks Victoria, who keeps snapping pictures while Lexie helps herself to a tea.

I smile, waiting for Victoria to agree. She *has* to agree.

But Victoria's only response is to snap another picture.

"Victoria?" I say. "What do you think of our house?"

Victoria lowers her camera. I want her to take another look, so I nod up toward the porch, covered in rainbow swirls and decorated with flower boxes filled with metal daisies. We just stand there staring at each other. *Why isn't she saying anything?*

"Come on, Lexie," Victoria finally mutters. "We should get the rest of the pictures done."

"The rest?" I ask.

"Sure. The whole neighborhood."

"You mean like Irma Jean's curtains!" I say. "And Harold's yard—"

"Right. We've got it. Thanks, Auggie."

Lexie slowly puts her apple down, half-finished, and she follows Victoria straight back toward the gate.

"Wait a minute," I try, because Mom hasn't even shown up yet, and the open house suddenly doesn't feel friendly at all.

Lexie and Victoria straddle their bikes, raise their kickstands, and take off.

But you liked it, I want to shout at Lexie.

"What was that?" I ask, turning toward Gus.

"I don't know, Little Sister," he says. "I'm not sure at all."

The two of them stop peddling in front of Irma Jean's house. When Victoria's flash hits the Pikes' front window, I notice the way the light settles into the giant crack down the glass.

· · · 26 · · ·

That Saturday, Gus and Weird Harold's dad rattle a couple of ladders against the Bradshaw place. In exchange for giving us their Monte Carlo, Gus has gathered some surplus shingles and has offered to help Mr. Bradshaw patch up the places where their old roof has started to shed shingles like hair.

I envy them being able to see the Bradshaws' garden and even Montgomery from so high up. I figure that from up there, the garden in the backyard must look the same way that fields of corn look from an airplane.

But Gus has a job for us on the ground—me and Weird Harold both. He's rigged a kind of pulley to raise and lower a bucket along the side of the Bradshaw house. When Gus and Mr. Bradshaw need a tool or some nails or a sandwich or a can of soda, Weird Harold and I put it in the metal bucket and shout, "Ready!" so Gus knows he can start pulling the bucket back up toward the roof.

It's all clicking along like a clock, until Gus calls down, "Auggie, I've got some screen in the back of Old Glory. You can take it across the street to Mrs. Shoemacker."

My stomach knots up because Mrs. Shoemacker sets me off balance. It's not like I'm really afraid of her. I just don't understand the way she stands in her front window, looking out at all of us.

"I need to help you here," I insist.

"Harold can help us," Gus says.

"She called you? She asked for screens?"

"Didn't have to call. You can see those screens around her front porch need help. Covered in holes.

Don't think the committee will like those holes much. Besides, it'd be a nice place to sit, if she didn't have to worry about bugs."

There's no arguing with Gus. So I head straight over to the house next door. Before I even climb the front steps, I can hear Mrs. Pike scolding Michael Nicholas for eating crayons. I step over Anna Beth, who's lying across the porch on her stomach, smearing on lipstick and staring at herself in a compact mirror, and knock on the door.

The chaotic music of the Pike house keeps trickling out onto the porch as I hear a flurry of stomping feet and voices calling out to Irma Jean, telling her she has company.

Her wide eyes fill the gray screen of the front door.

"Help me carry some screen to Mrs. Shoemacker?" I ask, pointing once over my shoulder.

Irma Jean makes a face as she crams the last of her peanut butter sandwich into her mouth. I figure she's going to start shaking her head as hard as her mom shakes dust out of the living room rugs. But she opens the door and steps outside, and I feel myself finally exhale. When my lungs fill up again, it's not just with air but with gratitude.

Together, we each grab an end of the roll of screen

108

from the back of Old Glory. "Have you heard anything?" Irma Jean asks.

"Not a squeak," I admit, because I know right off what she's talking about. It feels awful, not knowing for sure what Victoria really thought about the house. All that work, and now—a tight, uncomfortable quiet. The kind of quiet you feel your ears stretching through, like they're trying to go ahead and find the awful explosion that's bound to hit.

"Do you think you could call Lexie?" Irma Jean asks.

I don't think my voice is welcome on Lexie's phone anymore. But admitting it makes my chest feel squashed flat. So I act like I've really got to concentrate on keeping a good hold on the screen.

We knock on Mrs. Shoemacker's door, and hold our breath. Sure, she comes to Montgomery for church, and when she's in public, she looks as normal as anybody else. But this is her house. And the way she always throws her eye in between the slats in her venetian blinds tells me she keeps watch over it like a guard dog. I have this awful sinking feeling that when she answers my knock, it will be with a voice as vicious as a Rottweiler's, because all she wants is to be alone.

My legs get itchy, like they're begging me to run.

I'm ready to grant their wish when Mrs. Shoemacker shows up in the front door. It's the first time I've ever looked her square in the face. Now that I'm looking, she seems really young. Not much older than Anna Beth Pike.

When she sees us standing there on her step, happiness pops through Mrs. Shoemacker's eyes. Her grin makes her mouth look big enough to fit a whole loaf of bread inside it all at once.

"Girls!" she exclaims.

"We brought screen—for your porch—" I start, but she's already opening the door and ushering me and Irma Jean into a house that's got more pictures than Ms. Dillbeck's place. Only, instead of drawings, they're photos—of Mrs. Shoemacker and a man in a uniform.

She disappears into the kitchen, runs some water and clanks some mugs. "You two like hot chocolate, right?" she calls. Her microwave starts dinging as she punches its buttons.

I share a look of complete shock with Irma Jean as we prop the roll of screen against her living room wall.

"Do you two know yet what you're going to be for Halloween?" Mrs. Shoemacker shouts, her voice a little

too loud and a little too excited for such an everyday conversation. You'd think she was talking about going on a fancy vacation to Hot Springs—or the moon.

I'm so shocked. This isn't who I thought Mrs. Shoemacker was at all. But I manage to answer, "A mechanic. I'm going to smear grease on my face and wear a pair of Gus's grimiest zip-up coveralls."

"I'm going to be the Mad Hatter. I'm sewing the whole costume—even the hat!" Irma Jean says in such a happy way that it makes me wish, all over again, that I had a shine like hers. It'd be nice to wear something I could say I'd made myself, I think.

Mrs. Shoemacker's eyes are bright when she rushes back into the living room—until she sees me standing in front of one of her photos. Then it seems like somebody's dimmed her insides.

"My husband," she says, picking a small framed photo off the mantle. She runs her fingers down the gold buttons pictured on the front of the soldier's uniform. "He's overseas. Eight more months," she sighs. "Hey—the Bradshaws gave you their car, didn't they?"

I'm not even through nodding when she grabs my wrist. "I've got something for you, too—come here," she says, tugging me toward the back door. Outside, she points toward an arch at the front of a garden. The garden is beautiful, filled with pumpkins and gourds. Healthy and full of life.

"The arch," Mrs. Shoemacker says. "Could your grampa get that out of here?"

"Why?" I ask. "There's nothing wrong with it. Gus hauls away clunkers, and that doesn't even look old."

"It was a wedding present," Mrs. Shoemacker says. "I imagined, when I put it out here, that it'd get covered in vines and greenery. But nothing'll grow on it. Nothing but one vine," she says, pointing out the single green shoot curling up its side. "And you know that vine only ever had one flower on it?" She snorts a laugh. "One lonely vine. Seems like this thing's determined to remind me what life is like when you're married to a Marine."

I look up at Mrs. Shoemacker's face, which seems distant and sad. I feel kind of horrible for all the times I thought about her as our neighborhood ears. Mrs. Shoemacker wasn't eavesdropping on us as much as she was hoping she'd hear a way to jump into someone's conversation. And she wasn't shoving her face in between her venetians to keep us away. She was hoping that someone was about to come up her drive.

"I'll get rid of it," I tell Mrs. Shoemacker, nodding at

the arch. I actually want to do more than that. I want to change the arch, make it into something different. I'm just not sure how.

... 27 ...

Halloween comes and goes. My fat pillowcase of candy turns into a wad of empty wrappers. The construction paper black cats in Ms. Byron's classroom windows are replaced by construction paper turkeys.

In all, a whole week has to crawl by before I finally get the letter. Gus is off on one of his pickups, so I'm the only one home when the mail truck sputters by. I tug on the mailbox door and find an envelope—from the House Beautification Committee. *It's here,* I think. *Finally. The House Beautification Committee's going to award Gus and me for all our work. Those pictures from Victoria did the trick.*

My heart is kicking my ribs and my fingers are trembling as I tear into the envelope.

When I unfold the letter, I gasp and shout, "No! No, no, *no!*" Because this letter is the exact opposite of what I'd expected:

ATTENTION
AUGUST JONES

An Individual Residing at 779 Sunshine Street
Willow Grove, Missouri

The property at the above address is
currently in violation of the following
ordinances mandated by the city of
Willow Grove and enforced by the House
Beautification Committee:

1. The house located on the above property is
not being adequately maintained.

2. Recent updates are deemed substandard.

As the owner of this property, Mr. August
Jones shall have forty-five (45) days to
address these issues.

If the condition of the property does
not improve in that time, the House
Beautification Committee will enforce fines
for the prior forty-five (45) days and each
day the house remains in violation thereafter.

The amount of the fine will be determined
by committee vote and will be based on the
severity of the offense(s).

Thank you,

The House Beautification Committee
(Making our city beautiful, one house at a time.)

· · · 28 · · ·

I grab my bike and head straight for the wishing spot—
but it feels empty, because Lexie's not here, and Mom
never came for the open house, and now I've got a letter from the House Beautification Committee in my
pocket and eyes that are fogging up with tears.

They hated it. The words pour into my stomach and
harden, like concrete: they hated my house. *Some shine,*
I tell myself, the voice in my head sounding ugly, like a
chord played with a wrong note.

I leave Mom's billboard and head straight for Montgomery. I keep my fingers crossed the entire time that
Chuck will be there.

When I skid to a stop, I find the playground marked
off by yellow caution tape. I can't quite bear to look,

and I've stared to turn my bike around when I hear my name. With Montgomery being so empty, the sound is eerie, and it makes me shiver.

"Auggie!" the voice calls again.

I pull my eyes from the frayed laces of my tennis shoes and feel my entire body spread into a smile. I wipe my eyes with the back of my wrist, because I don't want to look upset in front of the man hurrying across the playground. "Mr. Gutz!" I shout.

His name makes him sound like a terrifying monster—some creature that rises from a swamp, covered in moss, his eyeballs and guts hanging by threads. But Mr. Gutz is no monster. He's a real-live man, with his eyeballs and insides right where they should be—a man with sparkling silver hair and kind eyes and a laugh that's always waiting to skip out from behind his lips. When I was still a student at Montgomery, he was my vice principal.

"Actually," Mr. Gutz says. "It's not Mr. Gutz anymore. My wife never liked it, so last summer, we changed our name to her maiden name. It was my anniversary present to her. It's Mr. Chong now."

My face falls. Chong is as nice a name as any, but it pinches me that Gutz is gone. It just seems like everything is losable—even a funny last name.

"What happened out here, anyway?" I ask.

"The House Beautification Committee roped it off," he says sadly. "I'm back to teaching again—over at Eastwood Elementary—and I came by after school to check in on the old place. I would have liked the playground equipment to be left alone, so that it could be used by all the neighborhood children. I hoped the families living in the area could use it as a park. But the equipment was already old, and it got knocked around in the storm. Since Hopewell is holding services here, the committee thought it would be best to keep everyone off the playground. Just as a precaution." He talks a little distantly, like the words coming out of his own mouth are still a shock to him.

"The House Beautification Committee," I grumble, shaking my head. The letter in my hand feels as heavy as a concrete block.

"Mr. Gutz—Chong—I—was hoping—Chuck—" I try, but my eyes are starting to get watery all over again.

"In the all-purpose room," he says. "Getting ready for the big rummage sale." He cocks his head to the side. "You okay, Auggie?"

I nod, but I don't feel okay at all. I race inside, where the entire all-purpose room is filled with tables, and the tables are piled high with stuff. A giant sign on

the back wall announces RUMMAGE SALE—PROCEEDS GO
TO THE REBUILDING OF THE HOPEWELL COMMUNITY CHURCH.

The squeak of my sneakers on the tile floor makes
him turn.

"Hey, Auggie," he says, but his face looks funny—a
little out-of-shape, like a washcloth right after all the
water's been wrung out of it.

I feel the same way.

"You've been collecting this stuff a long time," I
say. Because it's going to take me a minute to work
up the nerve to admit the real reason I've come to
talk to him.

"Longer than I'd initially hoped," he agrees.

"You got a lot of stuff," I tell him hopefully.

He only barely nods.

"It is," I insist. "A lot."

"Sure. But it's a rummage sale. A quarter here. A dime
there. Maybe a dollar every now and then." He shakes
his head. "You're right, Auggie. We got a lot of stuff."

The smile he tries to put on wobbles as he eyes me.
"What's the matter?"

"The House Beautification Committee has decided
they don't like my renovations."

I show him my letter. As he reads, he takes in a giant
breath of air, the way people do when they're shocked.

"Would you come take a look?" I ask, because if anyone can find something nice to say about our work, it would be Chuck.

He stares at the mounds of stuff and smiles weakly as he' offers, "I'll come look if you'll give me twenty minutes of sticker help."

••• 29 •••

"I've been meaning to come by, anyway," Chuck says, after I wound up helping him price the entire last table of clothes. "I've been meaning to, ah—"

"See what I did with your glass?" I finish.

"Yes—a little reinvention, I see," he says as we stop in front of my house.

"Maybe more like a demotion," I say.

"A demotion?" Chuck asks.

"Like when your boss gives you a job worse than the one you've already got because you've messed the first one up pretty bad."

"You didn't mess this up, Aug," Chuck says. "You did a really nice job."

"Yeah, but it used to be in a church, and now it's on somebody's old house."

"Church is a house. God's house," Chuck argues.

I shrug my way into an agreement. If anybody'd know for sure, it'd be Chuck.

"Do you really think we did a good job, Chuck? You don't think it's ugly? You don't think what we did is—wrong?"

He sighs. "I don't remember 'Thou shalt not paint thy house orange and green' being the Eleventh Commandment."

I laugh. "You know, you aren't as uptight as most ministers," I tell him. A glance at his shoes proves that much. "I guess we've done more than paint our shutters a funny color." I nod once at the spinning wind chimes we made from the Monte Carlo. "All of a sudden," I admit, "that letter from the House Beautification Committee makes me feel like working on the house was something really bad. Like I cheated on a test in school. Only, it still feels right, too."

As I scrunch up my face, trying to make sense of it all, Chuck's mouth stretches into a wide, proud smile. "That makes me remember your mom," he says, "and the time we set out to change the world."

···30···

"Maybe some adventures begin nobly," Chuck starts, eyeing the flowers on our roof. "Great knights and heroes climbing on their horses, ready to charge into battle. My adventure—the one I took with your mother when I was just a few years older than you are now—started out with hitchhiking."

My eyes go as big as oranges. I know I'm going to have to keep this story a secret from Gus. This is gearing up to be the kind of tale he'd hate for me to hear.

"I guess," Chuck goes on, "you reach a certain age, and you realize the world isn't much different than a house. You love your house—it's your comfort—but there are things you wish you could fix. The squeaky garage door, maybe, or the uneven kitchen floor. I know you understand what I'm talking about. The things in your house that drive you nuts.

"You get to a certain age, and you feel like you could fix things about the world, too. You think prejudice or unfairness could be done away with, same as a rotten floor."

"And Mom always had an itch to get out of Willow Grove," I jump in. Everyone says so.

"She said the place always looked drab to her," Chuck agrees. "Even when we were kids playing chicken on our bicycles. She always said she thought the place was kind of dingy, like a sink of old gray dishwater. She used to say it just like that." He chuckles.

"By high school," he goes on, "she was trying to brighten up all the dull hallways, filled with gray metal locker doors, with what she wore. She had this way of putting something together—even if the clothes weren't exactly fancy, on her they looked like a magazine spread. Gus used to always say she looked like she'd just stepped out of a bandbox. Everybody else just used to stare.

"Which was a big part of the reason why she dressed that way, no doubt about it. She liked the attention. Liked to push the limits—of anything, really. Always liked to test how far she could take something. She was always in the principal's office."

"Really?" I ask. "The principal?" No matter how wild everyone always swears she was, it's hard to imagine my own mother on one of those hard seats that are always propped up outside of a principal's door.

"You wouldn't believe how she knocked heads with

the principal," Chuck laughs. "Really challenged him, said he was picking on her. Even though she knew she was breaking the dress codes. As cockeyed as it sounds now, one day, she'd had enough, and decided it was finally time for the two of us to head off to change the world.

"According to your mom, we were always going to do it, anyway—change the world, I mean. According to her, we'd make our mark, and when we came back to Willow Grove, everyone here would see the error of their ways. They'd see that they should have let her wear her skirts any old way she wanted to."

"So you set off," I say, ready to hurry this story along.

"We set off," Chuck agrees. "Thumbs in the cool autumn air.

"Thing is, though, your mom—she was never really much of a planner. And you can't willy-nilly go about changing the world. The world's way too big for a couple of kids with no plan.

"We snagged a few rides," Chuck explains. "Got as far as Kansas City. Wound up turning back around when we ran out of hamburger money."

"Hamburger money?" I squeal, while Chuck starts laughing. He laughs so hard, his face starts turning as many shades as our front windows.

"You sure have had a crazy life for a minister," I say.

He laughs again. "Maybe so," he mumbles as Old Glory rambles into our gravel drive. He waves at Gus, who climbs out of the cab and starts rummaging around in the packed-tight bed of Old Glory.

Gus waves back.

"She did leave, though," I remind Chuck. "She did finally get out. For good. Everybody says Mom's in California, now. Shining brighter than the stars on the big screen or the ones in the sky."

Chuck's laughter dies. His face grows so dark, you'd think he hadn't laughed in about eighty years.

I stare at him, wondering, for the tiniest of seconds, if his stories aren't mostly made up, like the stories Weird Harold's dad keeps promising to tell me. But there's something so sweet about the way Chuck tells his tales. He never tries to paint himself up to be perfect, never makes himself out to be some flawless superhero. So his stories always feel like the truth.

Instead of walking straight into the house, like Gus normally would coming back from one of his pickups, he heads over to greet me and Chuck. I slide the letter from the House Beautification Committee into his hand and turn away, because I don't think I can stand what that letter is going to do to his face.

"Substandard," Gus repeats sadly.

Weird Harold appears, shaking his head and *tsk*ing us. "You're not the only ones," he says. "Ms. Dillbeck, Shoemacker, even the Pikes. They all got one."

"Everyone?" I ask, staring at the mailboxes lined down the street.

"Paranoid," Weird Harold mutters. "That first day, over at Montgomery. Everyone thought I was paranoid. We tried sugar with that open house of ours—and it didn't work. I should have stuck to my petition, before the committee had a chance to get out of hand. My dad and I are going to the city council meeting on Thursday. If the rest of you want out of this, I think you'd better show up, too."

I look up at Gus, feeling off balance. "Are we going, Gus?"

"Yeah," he says as our chimes start to clink in the breeze. "Yeah, we are, Little Sister."

· · · **31** · · ·

On Thursday, Weird Harold and his dad bum a ride across town in Old Glory. By the time we get to City Hall, we really have to cram ourselves inside the city council chambers, because the entirety of Serendipity

Place is already there. I wind up feeling like a folded-up piece of paper stuffed into a back pocket.

Victoria is seated in the first row, ahead of everyone in Serendipity. She keeps her eyes turned toward the table stretched in front of all of us, her eyes aimed right at her father, who is up there with the rest of the city council. Victoria stares calmly. At Victoria's side, Lexie keeps turning her head over her shoulder and eyeing the crowd. Her hair doesn't look so dangerous today; the spikes kind of droop, softening out. She catches my eye once, and whips back to face forward. After that, she doesn't turn around again.

We sit through the meeting, which stretches on so long, my legs start to go numb. I'm about to think it'll never end, when everyone on the city council takes a visibly deep breath, as though they've been dreading this very moment. The city council speaker finally announces, "We can open the floor to any new business," at which point, all of my Serendipity Place neighbors jump to their feet. So do I.

The room fills with so many groans and grunts that together, we sound like a lawnmower motor trying to kick over.

"I can't afford to fix my porch," Ms. Dillbeck says as she waves her notice.

"And I can't afford to replace all my screens," Mrs. Shoemacker pipes up. "What's wrong with using the screen my friends gave me for patches?"

When she glances my way, I give her a thumbs-up for speaking out.

"What's so bad about toys in the yard?" Mrs. Pike asks, shaking her own notice. "Says here that toys in the yard cannot exceed four. How am I supposed to keep track of my children's bicycles and rubber balls?"

"Now, now, now," Mr. Cole says, waving his hands in a way that says he wants us all to sit down.

"We have wind chimes and stained glass," Gus points out. "How can that be substandard? What's wrong with that?"

"We're in this together," Mr. Cole insists. "Certainly, in the interest of fairness, we would be happy to look at all your homes again. Reevaluate every single one."

This makes our groaning and clanking quiet down.

"What do you suggest we do while you reevaluate?" Mrs. Pike asks.

"Why, continue to work on your homes, of course," Mr. Cole says. "We wouldn't want to discourage you from that. We need to take a second look at the ordinances as well. Make sure we're interpreting them correctly. We want you all to know that we appreciate the fact that you're working on your homes. It's what we want you to do. But it will take us some time to reevaluate. Until after the holidays, surely."

When he smiles, I can't help thinking that he's got really long front teeth—like a wolf. I find my eyes searching for Weird Harold, wondering if he thinks it, too.

· · · 32 · · ·

When we step outside, we look like we've just come out of a fight. Chuck's been running his hands through his hair until it's turned into a rumpled mess. Gus's face is filled with so many worry wrinkles, it reminds me of the collar of a shirt that's been inside someone's fist.

The night has fallen, and the light from the parking lot lamp above us seems like some sort of shelter. We huddle under the light for a minute, the same way I used to rush under the eaves of Montgomery when it started to rain during recess.

"Whew," the Widow Hollis finally says. "A reevaluation."

Gus rubs his face, leaving behind shiny streaks of

worried sweat. "But they don't like what Auggie and I have done to the house. We're so far into this thing," he says. "Me and Auggie. We've got flowers nailed into our roof. We've got concrete on our porch posts. How are we ever going to undo—"

"Undo!" I exclaim, my surprise making my voice too loud. I clear my throat and try again, quieter this time. "Why would we ever undo it?"

"Because, Auggie, they already told us it was substandard," Gus says.

"And my swing set," Mrs. Pike moans. "They said the same thing about it, too. Said it was substandard. But my kids love that swing set. What will they play on, with no toys, no swing . . ."

"My porch," Ms. Dillbeck chimes in. "How am I supposed to do anything to make my porch look better—other than flat out replace it? Where am I supposed to find the money to do that?"

"Why would you need—" I feel myself begging for an answer. The idea of taking down the work I've done with Gus makes me feel awful—like somebody's just insisted I tear up a picture of my mom.

"They said they'd reevaluate," I try to remind everyone. "Didn't you hear them? We don't have to undo our improvements."

"Yeah," Weird Harold says. "But the same eyes are going to take that second look."

"So it's up to us," I tell him. "It's up to us to *make* them see us differently. We've got to make sure we show off our improvements in a way that means the committee has no choice but to see our houses as beautiful. We could do that, right?"

Gus and Dillbeck and Shoemacker and Harold shuffle, look away, like they all know I'm wrong, but don't have the guts to tell me so.

"Come on," I plead. "When Gus and I started making our flowers out of the Bradshaw car, it wasn't always pretty. At first, when we were taking the car apart, it was a real mess. Pieces of metal everywhere. We had to weld a whole flower together before it stopped looking like a big pile of clutter."

"So?" Harold asks with a shrug.

I grin, because this is the first time in my life that I can see an answer that Harold can't. "So, maybe we're just not finished yet," I explain. "Maybe Gus and I aren't done sprucing up our house. Maybe you and your dad aren't quite finished with your yard yet. Maybe the curtains in the Pikes' front window weren't enough. I'm sure if we all think about our houses, we could come up with new ways to really play up all the prettiest parts."

"Swing cushions," Irma Jean blurts. "If I sewed up some new cushions for the wooden swing, it would make the old set look better."

"Yes!" I shout.

"We could smooth out the old gardens," Harold admits. "Dad and I were in such a rush to get those plants in the back, we didn't do much to smooth out the old rows in the front yard."

"I could spiff up the porch," Dillbeck says, "if Gus could bring me some of that free paint."

"Chuck," I say. "What do *you* think is really beautiful? Like the most beautiful thing in the whole world?"

He smiles as he thinks a minute—I'd expected him to give us an idea for decorating. But now, the look on his face has me convinced he's thinking of a sunset or a baby, or maybe even the way Hopewell looked before the storm. After a pause, he says, "You know, what makes me stop and catch my breath, every single time I see it, is my congregation."

"Really?"

Chuck nods. "It's the way their faces look while I'm standing there at the pulpit. They're all waiting for me to say something that will change everything— something that will make everything that's bad in their lives wash away."

I've got to file this away with the stories Chuck tells me about my mom, because it's too big to decide what I think about it now. "We need to keep working," I insist. "I swear, that's the thing that's going to change this whole mess. What's going to make *this* bad thing go away."

Irma Jean sticks out her hand, like she did back at Dickerson. I put my hand on top of hers, and Weird Harold follows. Slowly, after exchanging not-so-sure glances, so do Gus and Ms. Dillbeck, and Mrs. Shoe-macker, and the Widow Hollis. Our huddle makes me feel packed in tight and secure, like together we're a fist that could beat back anything.

The next afternoon, I plop my brown bag, filled with a meat-loaf sandwich, right down on the lunchroom table next to Irma Jean. She's wearing a hand-me-down sweater with another pair of jeans that have white circles around the ankles. It takes her an extra long time to embroider over the circles, so the two of us still have one pair of jeans each with the special hand-done stitches around each ankle. The neck of her sweater is stretched out and sloppy. It has an especially roughed-up look—like maybe it was even worn by a couple of Pikes before it made its way into Irma Jean's closet. I guess it would be pretty hard to cut up a sweater and stitch it back together in a new way.

"Auggie!" a voice cries out. When I turn, Victoria is waving me over. She's acting like a super puffer fish, all blown up, I figure, after last night's meeting. At her side, Lexie bristles.

I glance down at Irma Jean, who shrugs and motions for me to join them.

I get a worried knot in my stomach when I sit across from Victoria. She eyes my meat-loaf sandwich with pity just before opening her lunch box and peeling back the plastic lid on some prepackaged fruit.

My heart is drumming against a hard lump of anger. My legs are melting. And all I'm doing is sitting next to Victoria and my old best friend. On the opposite side of the lunchroom, Ms. Byron eyes us with her arms crossed over her chest like even she is expecting something rotten to happen.

"Auggie," Victoria says, using a paper napkin to wipe off some of the liquid she's splashed from her fruit cup onto her fingers. "I know you and your neighbors were upset last night, at the city council meeting. I wanted you to know that the committee's not out to get you. They—we—are trying to show you."

"Show me?"

Victoria cocks her head to the side and reaches out to pat my hand. I jerk away like she's got electricity flowing through her arms and her touch shocks me painfully.

"How to take care of your things. You have to fix something in an acceptable way. There should be standards, right?"

"Standards?" I screech. "How to take care?"

I glance across the table at Lexie, who stares at her own ham and cheese on white. She knows my heart is breaking. Still, she doesn't say a word.

At that moment, I remember the way my hands had looked with my neighbors' under the parking lot light, all piled up on top of each other, a team in it together. I imagine Gus and Shoemacker and Hollis and the Bradshaws and Dillbeck and the Pikes squeezing into a tight ball all around me. I feel like they're right here with me, all of them, nodding in agreement as I insist, "It's my house." When Victoria shrugs, I repeat, "It's *my* house. Mine and Gus's," I add. "Not yours. Why should I have to paint it the same shade everybody else does? Why should I have to keep clear glass in the windows? Why can't I reinvent my own house, if that's what I want to do?"

"But my father—"

"Your father and his committee are going to come back out to Serendipity Place, and they're going to see the work we're doing, and the fines are going to disappear," I snap.

"Auggie," Lexie starts, but Victoria eyes her in a way that makes her shove down whatever she was about to say.

"You know something, Victoria?" I go on. "You like to remind me that my house isn't as new as yours. Because it makes you feel good about yourself. That's all your stupid committee does. It sticks its tongue out at everybody in my neighborhood because our houses aren't as big or as fancy as yours." Remembering the plans my neighbors and I made the night before, I straighten my back and blurt, "You don't want me to work on my house, you don't want it to be different, because then it just might turn out to be better than yours."

"That's really what you think, *August Walter*?" she asks, using my full name in a way that rubs me raw.

"That's really what I think," I tell her.

Lexie flinches as I snatch up my lunch and head straight

back to a smiling Irma Jean. Right then, the matching white circles around our ankles don't seem like horrible things. They feel more like friendship bracelets.

• • • 34 • • •

For the rest of the afternoon, Chuck's words keep rolling through my head, like a song sung in a round. I keep thinking about how he told me the most beautiful thing in the world to him is a congregation. I scrawl the word over and over in big bubble letters in my notebook during reading hour. By the time Old Glory rattles up the Dickerson drive, I've got a plan swirling in my head about how to improve our own house.

"Sure is an ugly old patch of land," Gus agrees when we get home.

He scratches his chin, thinking the whole thing over as he stares at our scraggly front yard. By now, we've got hats on along with our fluffy winter coats—just the kind of thing that Victoria didn't think I owned on the first day—because the wind has turned mean. Wind used to be welcome, back in the miserable-hot summer months. Now, it's got teeth, and it's tearing at our skin like a hungry tiger.

"Imagine it," I say. "A whole yard full." Now that I'm talking about the plan, I'm too excited to care about the cold that's starting to sink through my clothes.

"But—a congregation?" Gus asks. "With pews and everything?"

"Not a congregation exactly," I say. "That was just the inspiration. More like—like a crowd, Gus. A crowd like you'd usually only find at a family reunion or a baseball game."

"Where are we going to get the supplies we need for a project that big?"

I feel one of those Cheshire cat grins spread through my cheeks.

· · · 35 · · ·

Mr. Gutz-Chong is surprised by our idea, and maybe a little unsure of it, too. At least, until Gus says, "Seems to me, that playground can't be roped off forever. Seems you're going to have to get someone to haul it all off— the swing sets and the slide and the jungle gyms and the teeter-totter. Something like that won't be cheap. But we'd be happy to take all of it off your hands for free."

At that point, Mr. Gutz-Chong's eyes open up like

a morning glory that's blooming on fast-forward. He takes the idea to the public school administrative center and comes back the next day with a thumbs-up.

The only way to get the playground equipment on the back of Old Glory is to take it apart first—a job so big that Irma Jean takes a break from stitching up swing cushions and the Bradshaws stop decorating their front porch with their home-grown pumpkins and gourds long enough to give us a hand.

I figure if I were helping Gus get some small hauling-off fee, business as usual, my back would ache and my knees would creak like screen doors. I'd be so sore, I'd start hobbling around like the Widow Hollis. But I'm not working for pennies. I'm not working for the chance to help Gus buy a few more groceries to stick in the Frigidaire that's older than my mom. I feel like I'm working for a chance to change minds—Victoria's, and everybody else's on the House Beautification Committee. Which means I'm working for a chance to change everything.

After Gus and I unload Old Glory, we start in on our version of a congregation that very Sunday afternoon.

"Look," I say, holding up two metal sticks that had once been the bars in the Montgomery jungle gym. "Arms!"

138

Gus nods. "Okay, all right," he says. "I can see where you're going." He tugs on his bottom lip, thinking.

I take hold of two more bars—these are connected by a big black joint. "And this," I say, "this can be a leg." I point at the black connecting joint. "This could even be a knee!"

Gus smiles. "You're onto something now, Auggie."

"And that," I say, pointing at the metal tongue of a slide. "We could cut a big circle out of that, see, Gus? And then we could cut little slits in the circle for eyes, and a big round hole for a mouth—because this person, Gus, is laughing out loud. This one just can't even stop. Because Irma Jean has told her a joke. So her arms have to come around so that it looks like she's holding her stomach. It's got to look like she's got a cramp, she's been laughing so long. Okay?"

The next few days, Gus and I fill our scraggly front yard with people sitting and standing, some with their arms bent and their feet apart because they're running laps in gym class. As we build, I rely on all the things I've seen in Serendipity Place, at Hopewell, at Montgomery.

As Gus's torch hisses, I think about the last story Chuck told me, about changing the world. How sometimes the world is like your house. Only, I think maybe

139

my *house* could become more and more like the *world*. The world as I want to see it, anyway, with people who are laughing and skipping and running. In my yard, people don't lose friends or wear jeans with circles around the ankles. In my yard, mothers don't name their daughter after her grandfather and then dump her on a doorstep. In my yard, everyone is brave enough to stare down a snake. Only, there's no need for bravery, because there's not a single shred of unfairness to stand up to.

One afternoon, I hook little springs to the side of a lady's head. "Earrings," I say. Just the kind of enormous, fancy earrings I would wear if Gus had let me get my ears pierced.

To Gus, it's as though I've challenged him: *I dare you to come up with something better.* So he sets about figuring out a way to bend metal to make shirt collars or rippling neckties. He winks at me as if to say, *Okay, Ms. Smarty-pants, top that.*

I figure the woman in our yard who has a long braid would like a ribbon at the end—the same way my braids are sometimes tied in ribbons, on special occasions. Once I add the ribbon I've made from wire, I cross my arms over my chest as if to say, *What else you got?*

Gus chuckles and rushes back to the shed, where he finds a way to balance a person on his hands so that he's doing a handstand.

I grab a brush and start to paint makeup on ladies' faces. Add the rouge and lipstick I'm not yet allowed to wear myself. As I paint it, I imagine what it must be like to get to wear something as grown-up as mascara.

"Okay, okay, Little Sister," Gus says. By now, all the grocery stores in town are advertising specials on Thanksgiving turkeys and the malls are already starting to set up booths where early Christmas shoppers can get free gift wrapping. "What do you say we call it a tie?" Gus asks.

"Only because we're getting close to the holiday season, and I'm feeling charitable," I say.

"Oh, really?" Gus says, before twisting his face into a tease.

"Little Sister," he adds, "did you ever notice that all our people here are grown-ups?"

"Actually, now that you mention it . . ." I say as I look around at all the people in our front yard. I'd just liked the fact that all our figures had turned out to be so big and impossible to miss.

"I think that it's about time to expand our crowd,

Auggie. Time to add some kids in here—some folks your own age."

"Yeah," I agree. "Time for me to have some company of my own."

Gus chuckles. "I like that," he admits. "Company."

Together, we invent boy and girl figures, and this time, we use some of the broken objects from Gus's pickups to give each one of them some sort of prop. Some little clue as to what kind of personality each one of them has. One girl—the biggest brainiac in her class—has her face completely buried in a book. Another girl—a real motormouth, who is always spreading rumors—is talking on a cell phone. A boy who dreams of taking pictures of celebrities someday is aiming an old camera with an enormous flash—a Brownie, Gus called it—getting ready to snap a picture of the girl with the phone. On the opposite side of the yard, we put up a boy who is always hungry for new music, pressing a transistor radio to his ear. We create a girl who reminds me a lot of Anna Beth Pike, holding up a mirror while putting on lipstick. We've even got a boy who loves cartoons, who's stretched out on his belly in front of an old TV.

Weird Harold's got a pretty funny look on his face, the whole time we're working. His shirts are always

142

buttoned wrong, and his glasses are smeared, and his hats sit at crooked tilts on the top of his head. He looks like he did at the beginning of the school year, when he got so upset about licensing bikes.

To make him feel better, I put together a boy with a giant lightbulb over his head—he's even wearing a ball cap. I'm pretty sure that as smart as he is, Weird Harold will know he's the inspiration behind it—the boy with the bright idea.

Each day, we seem to have less and less of a yard, and more and more smiling faces. More mouths open with laughter. Just looking at my yard is like getting a hug.

··· 36 ···

"Forgot the secret ingredient," Gus announces as he shrugs into his coat. He thinks I'd be grossed out by the fact that he puts oysters in his Thanksgiving Day turkey dressing, and would refuse to eat it. Little does he know, I've been onto his secret ingredient since the second grade.

"Better hurry," I warn him. "The Super Saver closes early for the holiday."

Gus is still trying to keep those oysters under wraps,

so I don't even ask if I can come along. I follow him only as far as the front porch and wave as Old Glory chugs down the street.

"Dear Mom," I scrawl in the first page of my notebook, after plopping down on the first step. I lift my head, staring at the billboard looming in the distance as I try to figure out how to tell Mom about the metal flowers and the wind chimes and the company, how to describe the special way the outside of the house makes me feel.

A smile spreads as I imagine it—that face on the billboard finally stepping back through the front gate. I'll never give up hoping Mom will come back, the same way I'll never give up hoping the House Beautification Committee will change its mind.

I might catch a mini tongue-lashing from Gus when he comes home and realizes that I've spent his whole shopping trip outside—it is late November, after all—but the sun is bright and I love the noise and the look of our yard. The figures Gus and I keep adding to our yard give me comfort, the same way I figure Hopewell gives Chuck maybe a little more comfort than the rest of us, since it's a little bit more his church than anybody's.

I trace the "Dear Mom" at the top of my page with

the tip of my finger, unsure how to go on with the rest of my letter, when a strange man shows up, out of nowhere. Even though he's at a distance, leaning against our fence, I can tell he's staring at some of the figures in our yard.

He opens up our gate and walks right in, like it's public property—maybe a park, and everyone is welcome. He slowly starts to make his way down the front walk, eyeing the last figure Gus and I made—the one I like the most right now. When Gus brought home an old sewing machine and table from one of his pickups, I knew we had to twist playground equipment into a figure that looked like Irma Jean so we could sit her hunched down behind it, her tongue stuck out in concentration as she sewed.

He gets close enough to lean forward and sniff the bachelor's buttons, snapdragons, and lilies in our flower beds, which were all made out of Burton's broken waffle iron and turntable and ice crusher and griddle.

When he pauses by the porch posts that Gus and I have covered in QUIKRETE and Ms. Dillbeck's broken pottery, I realize he's the kind of man who looks like he dresses up every day—like he wears church slacks on Tuesday. Same as Mr. Cole or Victoria. But there's a softness about him, too—a sort of gentle feeling I've never gotten from either of the Coles.

He adjusts his glasses when he sees me on the porch. "Did you make all this?" he asks, pointing at the house, the yard.

"It was my idea to make it all. And I came up with some suggestions about how the flowers and the figures would all go together. But my grampa, Gus, is the one who knows how to use the cutting and welding torches. He lets me help cut pieces apart and stick them together every once in a while—but only when he's around."

"My name's T. Walker Doyle," the man finally says, extending his hand.

It's the first time anyone's ever offered to shake my hand—and it honestly seems a pretty strange thing to do, until he adds, "Ms. Dillbeck's nephew."

"The art buyer," I say, remembering all the pictures in Ms. Dillbeck's house.

"Museum owner," he corrects.

"I'm Auggie," I say, giving his arm a few good, strong pumps.

"Quite a handshake you've got there, Auggie," T. Walker says. I'm pretty sure it's a little rude to think of him by anything other than Mr. Doyle, but T. Walker has such a neat ring to it, I instantly latch onto it.

"You don't have the same kind of pictures hanging up in your museum that you send to your aunt, do you?" I ask, remembering the funny drawings.

"Of course I do," T. Walker tells me.

When I feel my face scrunching up, he asks, "Why wouldn't I?"

"They're kind of—not so good," I tell him.

"Good's a pretty funny word," T. Walker says. "Never seems to have the same meaning to any two people."

While I try to think this over, he goes on, "The artists in my museum have never had any kind of formal training. They've never been taught how to paint like some of the famous artists you see in other museums. But that's why I love them. Their art feels more honest to me because it's not coming out of their heads, it's coming out of their hearts."

That's an awful lot to try to cram into my mind all at once. I'm going to have to think on it a while before I really know how I feel about what T. Walker's just said. So I switch up the subject a little when I say, "I think these old pieces of pottery were yours," and point at the post beside me.

"That's part of the reason I stopped by," T. Walker says. "My aunt told me that everyone in the neighborhood was working to improve their houses. She's spiffed up her own place with a nice new welcome mat and some additions to her rock garden. But when she told me about your house, I had to use Thanksgiving to come for a visit—my first visit to my aunt's house in years. I had to see it for myself. I have to say that your house is just . . ."

I hold my breath a minute, waiting for him to finish.

"Incredible, actually. I'm really impressed with you, Auggie. Best house in all of Serendipity Place."

I get a grin that shines brighter than a searchlight. Now, I know exactly what I want to put in my letter to Mom.

I tell Gus all about T. Walker as soon as he gets back from the store, my voice bouncing around excitedly like a girl playing hopscotch. I follow him into the kitchen, pretending not to look when he pulls the oysters out of the brown paper sack.

"T. Walker's got me thinking about leftovers," I admit.

"Leftovers?" Gus asks. "Little Sister, we haven't even cooked dinner yet."

"We always have leftovers," I remind him. "I bet Ms. Dillbeck and her nephew will, too, since it's just the two of them."

I bring Gus to our window, and point through a pane of fuchsia straight toward Mrs. Shoemacker's house. Then I point to the Widow Hollis's house. "Not a single car of visitors," I point out. "And I bet Harold and his dad are eating by themselves tonight, too. The only people around here who have a bunch of visitors are the Pikes—two extra cars from two sets of grandparents. So they're taken care of. They won't even have so much as a single green bean left over, I bet. But here we are, a couple of people who are getting ready to have a *ton* of leftovers. Same as the Bradshaws, and the widow, and Dillbeck . . ."

Gus winks at me, because he knows I already have a plan. I race into the street, which is filled with fire-colored leaves raining onto the sidewalks and the earthy-sweet smell of chimney smoke and compost.

I make the rounds in our neighborhood, extending invitations. Nobody wants to come empty-handed, and it turns out everyone has the supplies right there in their pantries to whip up their specialties—since they were planning on making them for their own Thanksgiving suppers, anyway. When the Widow Hollis tells me she can stir up sweet potatoes until they're as smooth as whipped cream, I almost start slobbering right there on her front door.

The only one who doesn't really have a special dish is Mrs. Shoemacker.

"But you've got a dining room, right?" I remind her, which makes her face open up like it did when she saw me and Irma Jean bringing the roll of screen to her house.

We gather in Mrs. Shoemacker's dining room, filled with all the new silver and china that were gifts at her wedding and that she's never had a chance to use yet. Gus and I bring turkey and dressing, and the Widow Hollis brings her great-grandson and her sweet potatoes and her homemade rolls. Ms. Dillbeck brings the pies she'd already baked for herself and her nephew—pumpkin and pecan—and Weird Harold and his dad bring all sorts of vegetables—green beans and zucchini and Brussels sprouts and radishes and carrots and peppers—grown right in their yard. Some of their vegetables have been pickled, and some come in steaming dishes.

"Grab a seat, grab a seat," Mrs. Shoemacker shouts, which makes the china and the silver and the dining room and our Sunday best feel a little less formal. We all jump into action, throwing back chairs, plopping napkins into laps, snatching up serving spoons.

"You have to try the dressing," I insist. "You'll never guess what Gus puts in it!"

His shocked face makes the dining room burst open

with more laughter than I've ever heard in the cafeteria at Dickerson. It feels good to have brought all the happy voices to Mrs. Shoemacker's house, tangled up like the vines she'd once hoped would grow on her arch.

"T. Walker?" I ask, once everyone's started to reach for serving bowls. He's sitting in a chair next to his aunt, staring through Mrs. Shoemacker's front window. I wave the bowl of dressing at him. "Don't you want to try it?"

He finally pulls his eyes away, smiles as he grabs the spoon standing at attention in the mound of Gus's stuffing. When I glance through Mrs. Shoemacker's window and realize he's been staring right at the "company" in my yard, I feel like I've been given an extra helping of happiness.

· · · **37** · · ·

Gus doesn't have any pickups during the holiday weekend, so he spends every morning taking an extra-long time with the paper, sucking on his grapefruit halves, and sipping a whole pot of coffee. It makes me giggle a couple of times, the way he acts like a king during long holidays like this one, almost like he's pretending to be some rich guy who has nothing to do but wait for somebody else to come clean up after him.

"Isn't this the girl in your class, Auggie?" Gus says, sliding the paper across the table.

Victoria is splashed across the front of the Local page. My stomach sinks in on itself as I read about how Victoria is a junior House Beautification member, and how special she is. How she takes pictures of houses and brings them back to her father and the committee, how interested she is in the whole process of making her town beautiful.

I start to feel small. My skin starts looking like mud all over again.

I think about the driveways all over town—and beyond. I wonder how far the paper could go. All over the world, surely. Anybody who wants to read it could, I figure. Not just the town of Willow Grove. I wonder if Mom subscribes to find out what's going on in her old hometown. All the warm feelings I got from earlier in the weekend are suddenly behind my shoulder, like an item far away, in Old Glory's rearview mirror.

"I'll show you, *Victoria*," I mutter viciously as I pace through the house, trying to think of something new to add. Something that will really blow everyone

152

away. I head to the welding shed, where Gus and I are storing Mrs. Shoemacker's arch. But the just-right idea for what I can do to make that arch new is playing hide-and-seek with me, doing a good job of staying hidden.

Besides, I think as I head back inside, to make the house look really special, really different, I need some brand-new materials.

I grab hold of the hall closet door handle and yank so hard, I think I could snap my fingers into dozens of tiny little pieces. Gus never locks any of the rooms inside our house. Not even the bathroom. So for this closet to have always been locked, I figure there must be something *really* incredible inside it. Something that needs protection, the same way Gus protects the two of us at night by twisting the dead bolt on our front door.

But it's locked up tight. Same as always. The tarnished knob doesn't even so much as wiggle. I drop down to my knees and try to squint into the keyhole. But all I see on the other side is darkness.

"Little Sister!" Gus shouts. His voice sounds like an alarm I've just tripped.

I jump about four feet into the air.

"I was looking for new supplies," I stammer, shrinking away from Gus's angry tone. "Better supplies.

Supplies that don't look like playground equipment."

"Why?"

"Because—we have to have something *special,* Gus. Something important."

"What's bringing *this* on?" Gus's annoyance at finding me by the closet door is still making his face look as rough to the touch as concrete.

"The article. In the paper. About Victoria," I confess.

This softens Gus right up—turns him into a regular baby blanket.

"Come on," he says. "I think I know where we can get what you're looking for."

Gus and I head to the Widow Hollis's house. His knock brings her dandelion-seed head to the doorway.

"I already gave my best stuff to Chuck, for the rummage sale," she admits as we follow her slow limp around the corner of her house, straight for the garage in the backyard. "But if there's anything in here you want for your renovations," she adds as she unlocks the door, "it's yours."

The garage is packed with old dressers and bed rails and antique oil cans and picture frames and tennis rackets and clothing and dishes and jewelry and wire skeletons of old lamp shades. Porcelain-faced dolls and wooden pull toys and old tires.

"Widow Hollis, there sure is a whole lot of life out here," Gus says, looking about the garage.

"I know it—that's the problem," she says. "Too much life behind me, not enough in front. After a while, you don't want to think that way anymore. I'd rather have something to look forward to. Know what I mean?" she asks as she stares at Noah, her great-grandson, who is wiggling through the stacks in the garage like a mouse looking for a place to build a nest.

She looks at Noah with so many wishes in her eyes that I feel myself melting a little inside.

"It'll take us an awful long time to empty this place out. Not sure where Auggie and I would store all the things we could use," Gus says as I pick up some sort of tiny little motor, all rusted shut, from a shelf on an old metal cabinet.

"Oh, don't worry about it," she answers, tossing her hand at Gus. "You can come peel me off anytime you need some new supplies. Long as I can get a few jobs done here and there in return."

My eyes dart up at Gus. He smiles back at me. He knows that looking at the supplies has already given me a dozen ideas for new projects.

"Gus!" I shout, racing toward the house with the old motor in my hand. "Can you make this thing work again? Think about how it could make our company come to life!"

While Gus is busy trying to figure out how to make the Widow Hollis's old motors—gas *and* electric motors, from lawn mowers and vacuum cleaners and carousel microwaves and Weedwackers—cough back into working order, I use springs from her garage to add leaves to flowers and antennae to a giant new monarch butterfly that both ripple when the winter wind skips past.

We're attaching the butterfly to the bouquet on the chimney when Lexie and Victoria ride by, their bicycle tires making gravel pop. When Victoria and Lexie pause to eyeball our latest additions, I remember that we're getting deep into December, closer to the reevaluation the House Beautification Committee promised. And I feel like the time I have left to work on my house is too small— like a crowded elevator, filled with hard walls and elbows and umbrellas that jab your ribs if you're not careful.

As soon as Gus lets out a triumphant whoop, announcing that he's figured out how to raise the Widow Hollis's motors back from the dead, I jump at the chance to start dreaming up new figures—powered by far more than just the wind, this time.

Together, we make a girl who's wearing a wig as silky and straight and perfect as Victoria's hair, and her little motor allows her to constantly twirl her hair around her finger. We make a man sitting on an old bicycle—like Weird Harold's dad—and hook up a motor that makes his feet turn the pedals. We make two people with napkins tucked into the tops of their shirts, who are fighting over a wishbone; motors make their arms shift back and forth in their struggle.

My favorite of all our moving people are the three girls who are jumping rope, because looking at them reminds me of recess. Two girls are holding the ends of the long rope, and their motors constantly raise their arms up and down while the third girl waits for the perfect moment to come racing in. I can almost hear the songs they'd chant while jumping.

As time marches still closer to Christmas, Gus and I add white lights to the railing on our porch and a wreath with a red bow to the gate on our fence. The rest of

157

the neighbors stop sprucing up their own houses long enough to light candles in their windows. They put down hammers and drills and pick up knitting needles in order to make mufflers for gifts. They pick up whisks to stir cookies, glue guns to make ornaments.

Irma Jean sews about twenty red felt hats, like the one Santa wears. When I eye her, confused, she says, "For the figures in your yard," in a way that lets me and Gus both know how much she's been enjoying watching our yard come to life.

On Christmas Eve, I put on Mom's latest gift—a red velvet dress with long sleeves and a plaid sash—and Gus and I head to Montgomery, where the all-purpose room is completely decked out for the service. Chuck has even gone so far as to put up a Christmas tree, decorated with red ribbons and white lights. The smell of pine fills the room—it's almost the same smell as paint, I think. Like Montgomery has been fixed up, even though the school board said it would take too much money.

Chuck seems a little quiet tonight. But he brightens when he sees me and Gus. He shakes Gus's hand, and they share a few happy words about the holidays. When Gus asks, "Will we be seeing some rebuilding in the new year?" Chuck's face falls behind a shadow.

"I've tallied up the earnings from the rummage sale. But I'm still waiting to hear back from some businesses I've appealed to. Construction companies, that sort of thing," Chuck admits.

Chuck's tone gives me an awful off-kilter feeling. But before I can say anything to Gus about it, Chuck waves his arms, encouraging us all to come in close together, like a giant hug. Soon, we're standing, and we're all holding hands, and we're singing "O Holy Night." Everybody's voices blend together like drops of water, until the carol forms a river. As we're singing together, we float happily, straight toward Christmas day.

Gus and I unwrap our Christmas presents—new drawing paper and pencils for me, along with cologne that makes me feel grown-up and beautiful. And the new small toolbox I bought with my saved-up allowance for Gus—the one with the smooth wooden handle. And a picture I drew of the two of us, which looks a little like the pictures hanging in Ms. Dillbeck's hallway. I've put the picture in an old frame I found in the Widow Hollis's shed and painted up fresh, a different color on each side. Because everyone knows that pictures in frames are special.

Gus likes the picture the best and rushes to hang it in our living room, over the couch.

He keeps pausing to admire it the next few days, even as we're back up to our eyebrows in making new figures. He cocks his head and stares at it in a way that always makes *me* pause, because I love to watch Gus's face melt into pride and pure happiness.

As the year starts to behave like a windup toy grinding down to a halt, I hear a bicycle bell that makes me shove my face right in the window of our front room. Looking outside, I realize Lexie's leaning against our fence out front, staring at the Widow Hollis's old aluminum kitchen table, which is now the site of a birthday party—like the party I had back in the fourth grade. The entire table is surrounded by a group of friends, all of them with cone-shaped party hats on their heads. One boy at the table has a motor that raises his arm to his mouth as he eats a big triangle of pepperoni pizza. Another is blowing a noisemaker. Yet another is so into his birthday cake, he's got bright blobs of icing smeared all over his cheeks.

I wonder, for a moment, if Lexie recognizes herself at the table—she's the girl with the giant twists of wild, coiled rope for hair. I want to tell her, so I race out the front door.

She's so into looking at our company that she doesn't realize I'm standing on the porch.

I smile as her head moves from one area of the yard to the other, taking in the newest members of our company. She eyes a circle of kids sitting cross-legged, because they're in the midst of a round of duck, duck, goose. She stares at the boy made of old copper pipes, whose motor raises his body to his feet as he starts to chase the girl running at full speed, her pigtails flying behind her, because she has named him the "goose."

She stares, too, at the old corrugated tin we've used to create a group of girls holding hands as they jump around in a circle, because they're playing ring-around-the-rosy. And at the old chain-link fence and a whole collection of rusted tools we've used to build two teams who are having a tug-of-war with a thick rope.

Lexie tilts her head, eyeing a man and a woman we've made out of twisted bed rails, who have their arms wrapped around each other because they're dancing. And two coatracks that have become a couple holding hands, stacks of oil cans that are now the body of a boy who's whispering sweet confessions into a girl's ear—the girl who's listening has wide eyes and her lips are in a big round O because she's so surprised.

The way she eyes my work makes me feel even prettier, somehow, than my new dress from Mom did on Christmas Eve.

"Lexie!" I call as a flash causes both of us to jump. From the side of the yard, Victoria takes another picture, making her flash wash over our yard again.

"Hi, Auggie," Victoria calls as she drops her camera into her backpack and starts to peddle away.

Before she steers her own bike away from the house, Lexie's eyes go right back to the party at the table, and I swear, she zeroes in on the girl with the hair. I think she knows it's her. And she gets this look on her face—the kind of look I haven't seen since the two of us used to spend time at our wishing spot.

"It really looks like she's painting," Weird Harold tells me on the last day of winter break. He's leaning against our front gate, staring at our yard. His breath explodes out into the air as he talks.

"Thanks," I say, beaming like a thousand-watt lightbulb. Somehow, getting a compliment on my company is better than having a teacher tell me I'm clever, or

overhearing a couple of girls in the bathroom saying that I really am kind of pretty, despite my crazy hair.

The last person we added, just yesterday afternoon (the same one that Weird Harold is staring at in admiration), is a girl who loves to paint the outdoors. She's standing in front of an easel that holds a big tile with an outdoor design on it. Gus and I have put a piece of wood cut like an artist's palette in one of her hands and a paintbrush in the other. I've even added an old beret to the top of her head.

"I love the way that none of the people in your yard look like they've ever wanted to be anywhere else," Weird Harold says. It's the prettiest thing he's ever said to me. Right then, everything seems calm and perfect, for a little while.

But then, Harold nudges me. "You get your mail yet?"

The warm cocoa he'd put in my stomach turns into a popsicle. "Why?"

"It came. To my house," Harold confesses.

"The reevaluation?" I screech.

He nods.

"It's already come?" I remember the flash from Victoria's camera, and get hot and cold all over. I hadn't expected the reevaluation to be just another picture taken back to the committee. Somehow, I'd been expect-ing something loud and full of trumpets—like a parade.

He doesn't even get his entire second nod in when I start to race across the street, to our mailbox, where I find our own notice from the House Beautification Committee. My throat feels clamped off as I tear open the envelope:

ATTENTION
AUGUST JONES

An Individual Residing at 779 Sunshine Street
Willow Grove, Missouri

Following our reassessment, we have deemed the property located at the above address to be in violation of the following city ordinances:

1. Inoperable Machinery on Premises

2. Improper Maintenance of Property

3. Abundance of Trash on Property

The previous twenty-dollar ($20) per-day fines have accumulated to nine hundred dollars ($900).

Due to additional violations and recent accumulation of trash, Mr. August Jones, property owner, will hereby be fined one hundred dollars ($100) each day the property remains in violation.

Payment can be made at City Hall.

Thank you,

The House Beautification Committee
(Making our city beautiful, one house at a time.)

I feel sick. Trash? They think we live around *trash*?

I glance back at my front yard, at the painting girl that Harold had just been admiring. How can this be?

"Trash?" I ask Harold, finally managing to say the word out loud. "Trash is stacked up, piled high—like at McGunn's. How can figures like ours, that we've turned into something wonderful, be trash? And we *don't* have inoperable machinery—look! Our motors move! According to this, they even fined us during all that time they were reevaluating. How can that be fair?"

Weird Harold takes a deep breath. "You're finally starting to ask some of the right questions," he tells me.

$\cdots$ 40 $\cdots$

Our doorbell starts ringing like crazy early the next morning—the first day I'm headed back to school. It feels like a finger jabbing into my stomach, waking me from a sleep so deep I have to stagger down the stairs.

When I get to the open door and lean groggily against Gus's side, I find Mrs. Pike standing on our glittering walk in her chenille robe. "Have you *seen* this, Gus?" she asks, rattling her copy of the morning paper. On the front page of the Local section is a picture of our house. And the headline, "House Beautification Committee Targets Eyesores."

My shock over the story is a ripple that starts at the top of my head and races straight down to my toes. My eyes widen and my heart revs; I'm completely awake now.

"I got another note yesterday—*charging* us fines, this time," she says, crossing her arms over her chest. "I keep the toys in the garage. I painted the swing set. Irma Jean made new swing cushions and even some curtains for the little windows in our garage door. I don't know what they want. It's not like I can go buy brand-new everything."

I slide the paper out of Gus's hands. I groan, instantly too sick to my stomach to read so much as the first sentence. Because our house is pictured right there on the front page. And I wonder how Mom would ever want to come back to this, her childhood home being called an eyesore.

• • • 41 • • •

"I saw your house in the paper this morning," Victoria Cole spits at the back of my head later on the very same day. "I guess you saw it, too."

I try to pretend that I didn't really hear her. When Ms. Byron starts our science lesson, I sit up straight and proud, chin jutted out.

"Can anyone tell me what happens to a plant when its light source is blocked—say, by a fence?" Ms. Byron asks.

I throw my hand right up in the air. "It'll grow to the light," I say, tossing a glare at Victoria. "You can't cut a plant off from the light. It'll always grow right toward it."

Can't cut Auggie Jones off from the light, either, I think.

"Sure, sure. Everything's all fine and good until the neighbor chops the plant's head off because it's climbed the fence and is in his yard now," Victoria growls.

Lexie tries to shoot a "Shhhh" at Victoria.

"Besides," Victoria says, ignoring Lexie as she leans close to me, and whispers, too quietly for Ms. Byron to hear, "some flowers deserve to be leveled. Like, say, the flowers you've got on your roof. You go on, though, Auggie. You just keep on building up heaps of junk around your house. Like I said, it won't do you any good. Before you know it, that whole street will belong to the city."

"What are you talking about? You can't do that," I shout, too angry to care who hears. "You can't take our house. It's not something you could ever steal. It's not—a bike or a coat. It's a house."

Victoria narrows her eyes at me, starts to open her mouth.

"Girls," Ms. Byron snaps, popping a stomach pill into her mouth. "After school. My desk."

··· 42 ···

When the final bell rings, the rest of the class races off. Lexie waits for Victoria in the hall.

"Do you want me to tell Gus you'll be late?" Irma Jean asks when she pauses at my desk.

I cringe, shake my head. "I don't want Gus to know I'm in trouble," I say.

Irma Jean heads out to the hallway where she instantly starts pacing, shooting me worried looks every time she passes by the door.

While I drag myself up to Ms. Byron's desk, I picture Old Glory rattling horribly beyond the school's entrance. I picture Gus's eyes darting this way and that, wondering where I am as pretty new SUVs honk and drivers yell at him for blocking the way.

"Girls, I've been watching this feud from a distance," Ms. Byron scolds. "I've been trying to let the two of you handle it, but I'm telling you both now, this has to stop."

"I would, Ms. Byron," I insist, "but—"

Ms. Byron holds up her hand, shakes her head. "Auggie, that little argument this afternoon was uncalled for. It disrupted class. At the beginning of the year, I would have said it was unlike you to behave in such a way. But now, I have to say that your behavior is getting out of hand."

"*My* behavior?" I ask. "But she—she—" I stutter, pointing at Victoria. How can I possibly be the only one in trouble?

"I've been following the news story regarding the House Beautification Committee," Ms. Byron says. "I know Victoria is the junior member, and I know your neighborhood is having some troubles. Wasn't your house pictured in the paper?"

"Yes, but—but—" I try. Every word crumbles against my tongue.

"I think maybe you're taking your situation out on Victoria. It's not her fault that your house is in violation, Auggie."

"But, they—"

Ms. Byron eyes me in a way that makes me suck my words back into my mouth. I've never been this kind of girl before—not the kind who causes trouble. Not ever.

Just as my face heats up with shame, Ms. Byron adds, "Victoria, there's no need to bring your position on the House Beautification Committee into this classroom.

When you are in this room, you're Auggie's classmate. Understood?"

Ms. Byron lets up on the hard way she's staring at us. She nods her head once to excuse me and Victoria, and we both stomp out into the hallway.

I'm furious—it doesn't help that Ms. Byron got after Victoria, too. Because I feel like she actually agrees with Victoria. *Everyone* seems to agree with Victoria and the committee. I'm so mad that when I see Lexie I shout, "What's *with* you? Huh? Why are you so into Victoria? Did you ever once think about the fact that she's been going to school at Dickerson forever, but she doesn't seem to have a single friend here other than you? Why are you suddenly letting her make *your* mind up about everything?"

"Leave her alone," Victoria says, jumping in between me and Lexie. "You're just jealous."

"Jealous," I repeat, while Irma Jean stares at us all wide-eyed. "What you and your dad and this committee are doing isn't right," I hiss at Victoria. "It isn't right at all."

"You try to do something about it, *August Walter*," Victoria sneers. "You just try."

"Watch me," I spit back, determination burning as hot inside of me as the fiery spray from Gus's welding torch. "I will."

. . . 43 . . .

I'm not the only one whose anger is beginning to spread through her insides like poison ivy. The reevaluation and the story in the paper have both made the entire congregation of Hopewell so angry, they actually start shouting up at Chuck the minute he steps behind the pulpit on Sunday.

"We fixed it, Chuck!" Mr. Pike calls, from a seat in the back. "We picked up the toys in the yard. Irma Jean made new cushions for the swing set. But the committee *still* says the swing has been racking up fines now for more than two months. How can they do that?"

"Gus brought me all those shingles," Mr. Bradshaw adds, from his spot next to the piano up front. "Brought some to the Widow Hollis, too. Now, we hear patches are in violation? I can't afford the fines—so how am I supposed to afford a whole new roof?"

"It's pay fines or eat at my house," Mrs. Shoemacker agrees.

Chuck raises his hand to settle everyone down, and nods as he steps out from behind his pulpit.

172

"Why is *my* swing set in violation, when they've got old rusted pieces of the swing set from Montgomery cut up and glued together?" Mrs. Pike shouts, pointing at me and Gus.

"Now, don't start in on our house, Mrs. Pike. We're getting fined, too," Gus insists.

"I thought when they reevaluated our homes, it would fix the situation. But it's only made it worse," Ms. Dillbeck says. "Most of us can't exactly undo what we've already done. Once a porch is painted, you can't really *unpaint* it."

"You know Mr. Cole," the Widow Hollis tells Chuck. "You see him all the time downtown as you try to raise the money to rebuild Hopewell, don't you? Surely you can reason with him. You've got to tell him this isn't right."

Everybody starts shouting so loudly, Chuck has to stick his fingers in his mouth and whistle to get us all to quiet down.

"I'm every bit as concerned about this as you are," Chuck says. He sighs, leaning against the pulpit. He's looking as skinny as an old farm dog living on scraps.

"What are we going to do, Chuck?" Mrs. Pike demands. "We've got to think of something!"

Silence in the room swells.

173

"Chuck?" Mrs. Pike presses.

"Right now, I think your only concern should be for your homes," Chuck says. "I'll speak to Mr. Cole on your behalf. I'll certainly take your concerns straight to him, try to reason with him. But the most important thing right now is for us to stick together and support each other."

That doesn't sound like much of a solution—it sounds more like Chuck's trying to walk around the real answer. Everyone else must feel it, too, because we all just stare at him wide-eyed, waiting for more.

"I have to admit," Chuck says quietly, "that I am also at the end of my ideas." In our shock, Chuck goes on, "Our rummage sale didn't bring the amount of money I was hoping for. I've appealed to every appropriate business in town. But I've come up short."

"What are you saying?" Gus asks. He barely asks in a whisper, but the room is so quiet that Chuck still hears him.

"I don't have the money we need to fix Hopewell," he says sadly. "Everyone around here's facing hard times, and, well—I'm afraid—we might have to sell the property, and find ourselves another place to hold church permanently. We won't be able to use Montgomery forever."

There's such a quick intake of air that it feels like it's Montgomery that's gasped, not the people sitting inside the all-purpose room.

"Lose Hopewell?" Ms. Dillbeck blurts. "You can't let that happen, Chuck!"

Chuck opens his hands, to show us his palms. They're completely empty.

• • • 44 • • •

Gus doesn't look like he can quite wrap his brain around what Chuck has told him about the church. Because it's funny, really, how the brain and the heart are connected.

"Chuck is going to reason with Mr. Cole," I remind Gus, dragging him straight to the welding shed that weekend. "Remember? Chuck told me there was no Eleventh Commandment about how to fix up a house. Chuck will get through to the committee. Of course he will."

"Auggie," Gus says. "We tried. We gave it everything we had."

"Don't talk like it's over, Gus. When we're working on our company, I'm happier than any girl has ever been. And you are, too. I can see it in your face. Chuck sees that, too. Looking at our house makes him think of all sorts of stories to tell me about Mom."

"It does?" Gus asks, his face softening. "It reminds him of your mom," he mutters. The words haven't even completely fallen from his lips when he reaches for the welding torch. I grab a metal mask and slam it on over my face.

We use the Widow Hollis's old washer and dryer to make a boy with bright silver streamers coming out of his hand—a Fourth of July sparkler. An old vacuum cleaner motor allows a boy to dip his wand into a plastic bottle of soap. When the wind catches the wand, it looks as though he's blowing bubbles. We prop them in the porch swing and on the fence. We've got to be a little creative about where we put our figures, since our yard is starting to get so full.

We use some old bikes to put together a little boy who hangs from the front yard pin oak. His knees are hooked over the lowest limb, and he dangles upside down like a possum. He's got a big round stomach with a spring for a belly button, because he's an outie.

Our last two people turn out to be my all-time favorites: baseball players. The umpire wears a wire mask (made from an old screen door), and the batter is on his

176

belly, sliding toward an old plate that's anchored into the ground right in front of our gate . . . he's sliding toward "home."

"It brightens up the world," I tell Gus as we stand on the front walk, eyeing our creations. "Just like Mom wanted to do."

When Gus looks down at me, sadness and joy swirl through his face like the stripes on a peppermint candy.

• • • 45 • • •

Valentine's Day at Dickerson brings pretty much everything I've been expecting: brand-new plastic boxes on all the Dickerson kids' desks, and prettied-up homemade paper sacks with slits cut in them on my desk and Harold's and Irma Jean's. I swear, it's all so predictable.

But what bothers me the most is that Victoria gives me a Valentine. A pretty, fancy, store-bought Valentine with a little piece of foil-wrapped chocolate inside. Nothing like the small pieces of paper with hand-drawn crayon hearts that Irma Jean and I give out.

"What's the deal?" I ask Victoria. Because it's not like her to be nice for no reason. Especially to me.

Victoria shrugs. "Let's call it a parting gift."

"Parting gift? You moving, Victoria? Because I'm not going anywhere."

Victoria doesn't answer. She just grins.

The way Lexie squirms gives me an awful sick feeling deep in my gut.

By the time three o'clock rolls around, I'm feeling more than a little wonky inside. I don't even notice Gus when he lurches to a stop at the Dickerson door. Old Glory's got to honk to get my attention.

After we drop off Irma Jean and Weird Harold, Gus pulls Old Glory to a stop next to our mailbox. I glance to the side in time to watch Gus reach through the window to pull out a notice from the House Beautification Committee. And I get the same feeling I do when I have a nightmare of tumbling off a cliff—like I'm falling and falling without ever hitting anything.

ATTENTION
AUGUST JONES

An Individual Residing at 779 Sunshine Street
Willow Grove, Missouri

Refusal to repair the property at the above address has resulted in fines in the amount of $5,400 and climbing.

We have been forced to officially blight the property at the above address.

Other residents of Serendipity Place are in similar situations.

An emergency meeting will be held at City Hall tomorrow evening, at which time options will be presented to Serendipity Place residents in the interest of resolving the situation as quickly and as fairly as possible.

Thank you,

The House Beautification Committee
(Making our city beautiful, one house at a time.)

"Chuck didn't get through," Gus mumbles. "He couldn't reason with Mr. Cole."

His worry and mine feels far too big for us to hold. As we glance through the windshield, I swear that our worry is a black cloud that swells, growing darker, thicker, until it covers the entirety of Serendipity Place.

··· 46 ···

The very next night, City Hall feels prickly and so full of anger, I think the place might explode.

Voices roar, protesting, as the House Beautification Committee enters; Victoria's with them, wearing that smug look most kids get on their face when a teacher passes back an A.

"We all got your notice," Weird Harold's dad shouts, from somewhere off to the side. The room's so packed, I can't even see him in the midst of bodies.

"I'm glad," Mr. Cole says. He's no longer smiling and sweet. He's glaring at us, as though we've all done something wrong.

"We have listened to your concerns," he says. "We have reevaluated your homes. We have done everything we possibly could to make sure that you would be dealt with fairly. You did not comply with city ordinances. As a result, you have all acquired steep fines. It appears as though none of you has the ability to pay them. You've had ample opportunity to fix your homes."

"We did!" Gus shouts. "Mr. Cole, poor folks have poor ways, and sometimes, the only way to fix a broken window is with a tube of glue."

Mr. Cole shakes his head. "Improvements have to be made in an appropriate manner. We've told you all that, with our warnings. But in response, you all made your homes worse—patches on roofs, mismatched paint . . . it is *unacceptable*, Mr. Jones. We *have* to put a stop to the deterioration of Serendipity Place."

Before anyone has a chance to protest, Mr. Cole continues, "We want to be sure you understand your options at this point. The fines on your properties, now deemed blighted, will not disappear until you fix your homes in an acceptable manner. If you do not have the ability to pay your fines and make the necessary improvements, we encourage you to sell to the city of Willow Grove. The city is prepared to offer you a fair price for your properties."

The room groans—we've all been kicked in the teeth at the exact same moment.

"Fair price?" Gus shouts. "Fair means fair for you."

"Now, Mr. Jones—"

"Come on—these are blighted properties. You just said so," Gus insists.

"Yes. Mr. Jones. That's right. But—"

"Being blighted is going to dramatically affect the value of our houses," Gus says. He's got a look on his face like I've never seen before. I would bet my favorite front yard figures that Gus wants to swear—that he's holding the words inside.

"Take a deep breath, Gus, please," I whisper, because I've never seen Gus so upset in my life.

"I wouldn't pay full price for a house the city has blighted," Gus says, swallowing hard. "The city's not going to pay full price, either. We aren't exactly the richest people in town. Our homes are our biggest assets. The one thing we own that's worth more than any other. If you devalue our homes, we'll never have enough money to buy another one. None of us will."

"Mr. Jones," Victoria's dad says, trying to encourage him to calm down by making his voice sound as soothing as a lullaby. "Like I said, you had ample opportunity to fix your homes. You have forced us to take action."

It takes all the strength I can muster to keep breathing.

✳

Gus looks pretty sick to his stomach as he curls himself over his coffee cup the next morning. He slumps into a kitchen chair, elbow on the table and his stubble-covered chin in his palm. I figure he's trying to think

182

of a way out of this situation, so instead of disturbing him, I head out the front door, still dressed in my pajamas.

Mrs. Shoemacker's staring right at our house like she's been waiting for me when I step out of the front door. But she doesn't have a wide-eyed, open-mouth look on her face like she's happy to see me. Instead, her mouth droops and I think she might even be shaking a little.

I walk cautiously to the end of the drive, the gravel popping under my house shoes. When I pick up our paper, I instantly realize why Mrs. Shoemacker looks so upset. My house is pictured in the paper yet again, this time on page one, front and center.

The headline above the photo proclaims: "Blighted Neighborhood to Make Way for Community Center."

I start to shake all over. My nerves are like tiny Ping-Pong balls bouncing underneath my skin. "No," I mumble. "No, no, no!"

"The abundance of trash outside this residence is one example of the dilapidated conditions in Serendipity Place," the story reads. "Once the city acquires the houses in Serendipity Place, they will all be demolished along with the neighboring Montgomery Elementary, which has been vacant since the end of the last school year. . . ."

"Trash?" Why does that word keep showing up? It's the exact opposite of what I thought I was doing. The last thing I ever wanted anyone to say about my house.

And they're going to knock us down—knock us all down—right along with Montgomery Elementary.

I can hardly hold in everything I want to say to Victoria as the morning drags on. When Ms. Byron finally lets us out to recess, I race straight through the playground dust that Victoria and Lexie kick up with their shoes. They hop into swings, and I stand right in front of them, like a giant roadblock.

"I'm not going to leave without a fight, Victoria," I say through gritted teeth. "We've got rights, too."

"Oh, really? The right to be filthy little pigs?" Victoria snickers as she sways in her swing. She makes a little snort in the back of her throat and elbows Lexie, who's seated in the swing next to her. Lexie doesn't join Victoria in her laughter, though. Instead, she gives Victoria a rough glare.

"The right," I tell Victoria, "to decorate the way we

want to. The right to fix our own houses the way we see fit."

"Auggie, Auggie, Auggie," Victoria snickers. "Did you ever happen to notice that those—those—*things* in your yard are made of garbage? Ready for the scrap yard. Somebody else's used-up stuff. That's not decorating. That's turning your house into a junk heap."

"No—it's—reinventing," I protest.

When Victoria rolls her eyes, I go on, "What about everybody else on the street? Why are you going after them? If you don't like the way I decorate my house, fine. Come after me. Not the Widow Hollis and Weird Harold and Mrs. Shoemacker and Irma Jean's family. They're trying to patch what they have."

"When something breaks, it's trash," Victoria tells me. "A broken window or a ripped-up screen is trash. People shouldn't have trash on the front of their own house. Besides, your house is the *worst*—on the block, in the whole state, the entire country. It's got to be. Metal flowers on the roof? Heaps of junk all over your yard? Are you serious? If you cared so much about Serendipity Place, you wouldn't have a house like that. A house that ruins the whole neighborhood."

On the opposite side of the playground, Ms. Byron begins to slowly make her way toward me and Victoria. From this distance, I know she can't hear us. But she can surely tell, by the way we're leaning into each other, heads jutted forward, pointing, jabbing back and forth, that we're arguing. I can see the unhappiness etched into her face.

"You know something, Auggie?" Victoria says quietly, without any hint of sarcasm or anger. Almost like she's a teacher lecturing me. "What we've been asking isn't even really that big of a deal. If you painted your shutters all those different colors, why couldn't you find a way to paint them all one color? I think you like being poor." The word—*poor*—scratches. "You wear it like a badge," she goes on. "Because being poor means you don't have to play by the rules."

"The rules?" I say. "The rules should work for everybody, Victoria. No matter how much money you might have in the bank. Otherwise, the rules aren't right."

· · · **48** · · ·

We're eating off our TV trays in front of the news when our house starts to flash across the screen.

"When did they film this?" I ask Gus, clutching my stomach.

Gus only shakes his head.

"Well, I think they should clean that place up," a girl says. Not any girl, though—a girl from Ms. Byron's fifth-grade class. One of the Dickerson kids who have spent the year cringing at Old Glory. She looks straight into the camera when she talks, so it's like she's getting after me and Gus right here in our living room.

"It's awful," a boy says, dipping his head down so that he can speak into the reporter's microphone. That boy's face shocks me worse than a fraying electrical cord. Because he's *not* in Ms. Byron's class. I've never seen him before. Not ever. And I know our house has been in the paper—more than once, even—but I hadn't thought about everyone in town making up their minds about it without ever having met me or Gus. At that moment, the entirety of Willow Grove seems full of Victorias.

"Heck, I think they ought to leave Auggie and Gus alone," another boy shouts, yet another face I don't recognize. But he's got white circles on his jeans.

"I believe we're famous, Auggie," Gus says. He drops his knife onto his plate with a clank and droops into his favorite living room chair. He puts his TV tray to the side, which means he's done with supper. But he's hardly touched any of his food. In fact, his plate looks pretty much like it did when he sat down, except the cream gravy's not steaming anymore.

Seeing Gus so sad makes me put my knife down, too.

"Where do you stand on this issue?" the reporter asks a man in a suit jacket. I rub my forehead, because I already know what his answer will be. He'll say he hates our house. Because our city is divided right down the middle—between people like me who have worn jeans with white circles, and people who never have. The white-circle people side with me and Gus, and the ones who have the kind of clothes that could only hang in the closets of fancy new homes think that Gus and I have been asking for trouble all along.

"Well," the man begins. I've been so intent on staring at his suit instead of his face, it takes his name flashing along the bottom of the TV screen for me to realize who it is: *Edward Cole*. I clutch my stomach and groan. Victoria's standing at her father's side, staring seriously into the camera.

"As the head of the House Beautification Committee," Mr. Cole says, "I have always believed that the Joneses should be required to clean up their property. The Joneses have flown right in the face of everything our committee stands for. In fact, all the committee wanted in the beginning was for Mr. Jones to use clear glass to repair his windows. Instead, Mr. Jones brought heaps of broken and useless junk home and cluttered his roof and his lawn. Now, I'm a reasonable man. I know that Mr. Jones hauls trash for a living, but he certainly doesn't have to bring his work home with him."

"In fact," Victoria adds, flashing a beautiful, white-toothed smile for the camera, "the committee and I have a special name for the Jones house. Since it's completely covered in junk, and since it sits on a corner, we all call it the *junk-tion* of Sunshine and Lucky."

The reporter offers a chuckle.

"The Jones house is not the only property in Serendipity Place in violation of current codes," Mr. Cole goes on. "Because the residents have neglected their homes and refused to fully comply with repeated warnings, we have been forced to officially blight the entire area."

Gus groans and slumps over the worn-through arm on his chair, and I have to go outside to get a breath. That name that Victoria has given our house doesn't just sting, it kills. I feel my heart coming apart in my chest.

I stagger to the end of the yard, wishing for a way to dull this ache. I open the gate and stand on the sidewalk, feeling my lungs tighten with fear, until a tiny bicycle bell rings, a few feet down the street. When I look, Victoria is steering her bike in circles with one hand and holding a can of soda with the other.

"Judging by the way you look, I'd say you saw the news," Victoria taunts. "My father's going to clean up this neighborhood. He's going to replace all these run-down houses with a community center. He's going to make it so pretty. And then he's going to run for mayor. And then he's going to run for governor. And then I'm going to live in the governor's mansion."

She brings her bicycle to a stop at my curb and knocks her head back, emptying her soda can. "Here," she says, holding the can toward me. "For your house. While you still have one."

I narrow my eyes at her and knock the empty can into the street.

· · · **49** · · ·

"What are you going to do?" The words reach out the very next afternoon and tap my shoulder, gently. Gus has just dropped me and Irma Jean off after school, and I'm standing in the yard, staring up at my house.

When I turn, I find Irma Jean standing beside a figure—the one twirling her wig around her finger.

Her house is quiet, because her parents are surely at City Hall, which is also where Gus has gone almost every day for the past week. Everyone from Serendipity Place is trying to work something out, as though their words are actually hammers and wrenches with the power to fix this problem.

Irma Jean slides an old beat-up brown paper bag from her backpack. She pulls out a brownie as thick as two stacks of playing cards. "Go on," she says. "I was saving it for an after-school snack. Now you can have it."

The brownie makes my mouth water like a hose with a hole in it. Irma Jean doesn't think words at the City Hall are strong enough to save us. She wants to bribe me into telling her my secret plan.

I stare at Irma Jean's feet to keep from looking at her hopeful face. The grass is beginning to sprout green around the feet of every single figure. March feels like a fragile blue egg—only, instead of a bird that's crawling out, it's spring.

"Gus seemed like he was in an awful big hurry today," Irma Jean presses.

"Triple pickups," I say. "Spring cleaning's started."

"Is he still trying to get the money for the fines?"

"Yes," I sigh. "Yes, he's still trying to get the money for the fines."

"Do you think he'll get enough?" she asks, quietly.

Her words poke straight into my doubt. "Probably not," I admit.

Irma Jean shrinks. She uses the toe of her right sneaker to scratch her left ankle. I watch her toe move up and down over the white circle, thinking about how glad I'll be when it finally gets warm enough to wear shorts.

"Bet you've got another idea," she whispers. "Come on—tell me. I wish—" Irma Jean's voice gets real far off. "I wish I could help, you know?"

"You do?"

Irma Jean nods. "Honest."

"Okay. Okay, maybe," I say. "You could be my cover while I'm gone."

"Gone?"

I nod. "To California."

"California?"

"My mom's in California," I remind her. "Everyone says so."

"But what good is she going to do?" Irma Jean asks. "Are you sure she wants—" She stops short. "I mean, she left. Why would you think she'd want to see you now?"

192

A hard little lump of anger glows hot inside my chest. "She can help me," I insist defensively. "Besides, I write her letters all the time."

"Yeah, but does she answer?"

I make a face at Irma Jean that shows how much her question hurts. "Chuck told me this story about how he and Mom once tried to hitchhike, when they went out to change the world. So I'm going to hitchhike out to California," I explain.

"No, you're not," Irma Jean says, her mouth hanging open.

"I'm going to hitchhike out to California. And I'm going to bring Mom back so she'll help me stand up to that committee. Nobody in this whole world is braver than my mom, Irma Jean. She could stare down poisonous snakes. And when she was young, she wanted to change the world. If anybody can scare that stupid House Beautification Committee away, change things for the better, it's my mom."

Before Irma Jean can argue with me, I say again, "You can cover for me."

Irma Jean starts to turn a sickly green, right above the spot where her jean jacket hugs her neck. "I can?"

"Sure," I say, motioning for her to follow me toward my front door. "You can pretend I'm over at your house.

For a little while. Then, after I'm long gone, you can let Gus know that I'm okay. That I'm with my mom."

"I don't know," Irma Jean moans.

She's still whining as we weave between the figures that have completely crowded our front lawn. "I don't know, Auggie," she says again as she follows me inside my house.

I toss my books on the front hall table and head straight for the closet, in search of supplies for my trip. But the door is locked. Like always. Like I should have known it would be. But I give it a good kick just the same.

I head for Gus's room, where I tug his ancient suitcase out from behind his shoes. It's been so long since Gus has taken a vacation anywhere that when I open it, I find a dead spider who'd managed to crawl in through a crack. I dust her cobweb out with my hand, then drag the suitcase up to my room.

"This is so dangerous, Auggie," Irma Jean insists as I start tossing my early spring sweaters inside. "What if you get hurt?" she presses. "What if something happens?"

"Something *will* happen if I don't go, Irma Jean," I say, snapping the suitcase shut. "We'll lose our house. So will you. So will everyone in the neighborhood."

As I stomp down the stairs and out the front door, Irma Jean admits, "I don't like this." All the way to the corner, she whimpers like a left-behind dog.

"Irma Jean!" I snap. "I don't care if you like it or not. I can't do anything without a plan, all right? And getting my brave mom is my plan. So maybe it's not the most perfect plan in the world. But it's all I've got!"

··· 50 ···

Irma Jean's eyes are still pleading with me as I turn away. I throw my thumb right into the air to let all the drivers know that I need a lift. Instantly, tires squeal to a complete halt. Before I even look to see who's stopped for me, I tell Irma Jean, "I'll be back soon."

I've only started to reach for the door handle when a pair of hands clutches me by both shoulders and yanks me away.

"Hey," I moan as Irma Jean waves for the truck that's stopped to take off down the street again.

"You have to know how risky that is," she snaps at me.

"I have to do something," I shout. "We're going to be homeless, Irma Jean. All of us. I have to go get my mom. She's the only person I know who can fix this."

"Here," Irma Jean says, reaching into her backpack. She pulls out a wad of dollar bills.

"What's this?"

"My birthday money from my grandma and my aunt and uncle. I've been carrying it to school to keep Cody Daniel from stealing it. Use it as bus fare."

I feel a grateful ball of tears swell in the back of my throat.

"You think it's enough to get to California?" she asks.

I'm not sure it is, but she's so sweet to give me her birthday money, I nod like it's all I'd ever need in the world. I hug her a thank-you.

I head down to the corner bus stop. I sit on a bench, waiting, feeling as serious as a math teacher. I begin to wonder how I'll ever get to the West Coast. But then I figure if I keep changing buses, one after another, stop after stop, I'll get there.

When a bus sighs at the curb, I hoist my suitcase up the steps and slam some money into the slot. I hurry to a seat before the driver can question me.

I ride toward the edge of town—a quiet, lonely section where weeds grow up around the corners of abandoned factories and boarded-up filling stations, while the neon lights of liquor stores flicker angrily.

The bus ambles past the half-burned-out letters of a sign flashing VACANCY and a motel with a pool so filthy, it looks like a lake of motor oil.

We ride until a green CITY LIMITS sign looms large at the end of a broken sidewalk.

I figure this must be a good place to change buses, head from one city into another.

My suitcase bangs against my legs and the edge of the bus seats as I walk down the aisle toward the door. I'm still ready to find my mom. But I'm nowhere near California. Knowing how long it's taken to get to the edge of town makes California feel as far as the North Pole.

My heart pumps. I don't know when another bus will come by. What happens when I need to sleep?

I stand at the bus stop for what feels like months, feeling tiny and alone. The world is enormous around me, filled with shadows and mysteries and dangers.

As I tremble, terrified of the who-knows-what that lies ahead, a white car screeches to a stop next to my curb. And a man gets out and heads right toward me.

"Auggie!" Chuck shouts. As he stares at me, standing there with my suitcase, he begins to look like the kind of uptight preacher who would get after me for anything—not like someone who ran off with my mom, with the half-baked notion of changing the world.

"What are you doing here?" I ask. I know I haven't quite crossed over the city limits yet, but I feel a little like we're at the absolute end of the universe.

"Irma Jean came looking for me. She told me she gave you bus fare, but she got so worried, she asked me to come track you down. I've been driving to every single bus stop I could think of trying to find you." He's so relieved, he's actually panting. "Irma Jean wouldn't tell me what you were doing. Get in the car, Auggie. Tell me what this is about."

"You can't stop me," I tell him. "I'm going to get my mom. You know her better than anyone around here, except for maybe Gus. You told me yourself how brave she is."

"You think your mother's going to fix this mess?" he

198

asks. His face softens, darkens when he repeats, "Your mother."

"*She's* in California, so I'm going to California. She stood up to some dumb old snake, and she can stand up to that committee."

"This has gone too far," he mutters. "Come on. You want to see her? I'll take you to see her."

He slips the suitcase from my hand and puts me in his car. We drive down a narrow dirt street, snaking sideways so that the city limits sign remains behind us, but we don't ever leave town. We sort of straddle the line, one set of tires in Willow Grove, the other set outside, as we go farther and farther down the road.

"Chuck?" I ask, my blood speeding like a race car though my ears. "Where—where is she? Have you always known?"

By the time he finally stops, the whole world is trying to get dark. Kind of like the earth is so tired, her eyes are drooping shut.

"She was going to come back," Chuck says. He cuts the engine, but his headlights still wash over an old wrought-iron gate.

"Chuck?" I croak again, my heart throbbing like a finger that's been smashed in a door. "Chuck?" This can't be right. It can't. Because he didn't stop at a house. We're at the opposite of a house. We're at a cemetery. Mom can't be here. She can't.

"She was going to come back," he repeats, opening his car door and stepping outside.

"Back?" I repeat, stepping out, too. The wind's picked up a little, and it starts pulling my braids around and pushing Chuck's black coat back from his sides.

"We left together," he says, eyes on the sky as he takes a couple of steps toward the gate.

"Off to change the world," I say, my voice thick with fear. For some reason—maybe because I'm ready to leave this place—I drag my suitcase out with me. Its weight tugs so hard against my body that it feels like a rock dragging me underwater.

"No, we'd come back from that adventure. Not that it was really that much of an adventure. This trip—when we left for California—this was later. You had just been born."

"You were with her when I was born?" My voice cracks as I ask, "Are you—are—"

Chuck looks at me with shock. I figure he can see my hope floating around inside me, the same way you can see minnows swirling just under the surface of a lake. "I'm not your dad, Auggie."

"Then who—who—Gus would never say—who—"

"Don't think Gus ever really knew what to tell you, Auggie. Your dad was somebody who passed through town and then left, quick as he came. Even your mom never really said much about him. People used to think it was me. Maybe they still think it's me. I wish I was, Aug. More than anything. But I'm not.

"Having you, it changed her," Chuck says. "She wanted so much to be better. For you. After she had you, she was prettier than ever. More mature looking, I guess. She had started to get decent work close to home—modeling work—like that billboard she did for the dress shop. And she thought if she went to California, she'd get even more work. Better-paying work. Doing something big. As a real model. We all agreed that she should go.

"You were a baby, though, so she hesitated. Even though she wanted to go so badly. It was so obvious. Her mouth practically watered over the idea of California. As brave as she was, she wasn't sure, because of you.

"We'd already had so many adventures together, I thought, 'Why not one more?' So I said I'd go with her. All the way to California. Made it to the coast because this time we did have a plan: I'd get some crummy job, support us so she could spend all her time chasing her dream. We couldn't take you, though, because we wouldn't have time, not for a little baby. So we left you with Gus. He said he'd take care of you. And I'd take care of your mom. Just until she got started. When she had her own steady work, her own money, she'd come back for you."

"She gave me Gus's name because she needed to dump me," I challenge. "She needed to make sure Gus would take me."

"She wanted to tell Gus she was sorry for all those wild times," Chuck corrects me. "She wanted to show him that she loved him. Gus taking care of you was supposed to be temporary."

"Gus never told me this."

"He wanted to," Chuck says, taking a step toward the cemetery gate.

No, no, this can't be right. *No*, I think. *No*.

"She got work. Like we all thought she would. In California. Things were going so well. She had enough money to find a real nice place of her own. She wanted me to stay in California, quit my crummy job, and take care of you. Said she'd pay me to look after you."

I keep staring, my throat dry and my chest heaving as though all the air in the world isn't enough.

202

"She would have come back," Chuck says, still edging closer to the gate.

"Why—why didn't she?" I ask, but I know. Because of where we are. I already know.

"She got this job—catalog work—and she had to fly out for the shoot. Once the shoot was finished, she was going to come get you. Bring you out to California. I was busy moving her things into her new place. Setting up a room for you. But the plane—a private plane—they loaded it with too much stuff for the shoot. It was too heavy. The plane—just—it crashed."

I'm shaking. The suitcase slips from my fingers, hits the ground, pops open.

"But you had a plan," I say dumbly, snatching at anything I can to try to make this story untrue.

"We had a plan," Chuck agrees. "Not like the time we set out to change the world. It was a good plan. It was working. Her plan got snatched out from under her.

"I brought her ashes back," Chuck says. "Gus was so torn up, he couldn't deal with a big funeral. Could hardly deal with losing her right when she'd really started to get herself together. It was too much. So we scattered her ashes here. The two of us. On the line between leaving and not leaving. Because that was kind

 203

of where she lived, you know? Between wanting to go and wanting to come back to you. She didn't give you up, Aug."

"Why would Gus let me believe she was still alive?"

"Because you—when you were real little, you'd point to your mom's billboard, and Gus would say, 'That's your mom.' And it would happen more and more: you pointing to your mom, and Gus saying, 'That's her, shining up there like a star in the sky.'"

"Shining," I repeat.

"His tale started growing," Chuck goes on, "taking on a life of its own. Anytime somebody would hint at the truth of where your mom was, he'd pull them aside and tell them, 'Not yet. She doesn't know yet.' After a while, you know, it was like we needed to believe she was still alive, just like you did. Everybody in Serendipity Place. And me, too.

"The story was for us, Auggie, as much as it was for you. When any of us talked about her like she was still alive, then our bright shining star hadn't fallen. We needed her to be real. We needed to think that somebody from the old neighborhood really was out there shining like a star."

A lonely tear trails down my cheek.

"My life changed the day I helped Gus scatter

her ashes," Chuck admits. "Maybe, I thought, I could help other people who were straddling some line. Help them make a decision that would change the course of their lives. That was the day I decided to walk inside Hopewell. The day I decided to become a minister."

"But I write to her," I continue to protest. "I send her things. She sends me things back. That's proof that she's still alive. I don't care what you say."

"You need proof?" Chuck asks. His voice is soft, but his words are something you'd say to a person who'd accused you of lying.

Not lying, I want to tell Chuck. *Just mistaken. You've made a huge mistake. About all of it. She can't be gone. Not now.*

"Gus has your proof," Chuck says. He scoops my spilled clothes into my suitcase and tosses my things back into his car. Chuck pulls a cell phone from his pocket and calls Gus. He tells him we're on our way. He tells him I need to see the closet.

"The front hall closet?" I ask. "The closet Gus keeps locked?"

Chuck eyes me sideways, and we retrace the path I took across town. The longer the quiet drive stretches on, the tighter my skin feels.

When we get to my house, Gus races to Chuck's car

and throws open the door, relief washing down his face like a waterfall.

"Is it true?" I ask him.

"True?" he asks, looking past me, at Chuck.

"It was time, Gus," Chuck tells him.

"The closet," I say, pushing past Gus and heading up the walk. "Unlock the closet, Gus!"

He shakes his head, but the look he gives me is one of utter defeat. He walks inside; I feel like the whole world is beating a million different drums, all to the exact same beat. And the key is in his hand. And he's opening the closet door. And everything inside is tumbling onto the hall floor. Envelopes fall like snowflakes. A few brown paper packages fall, too. I reach down, touch the edge of an envelope. It says, "Mom," in my writing. Every letter I've ever written. Every present I ever tried to send.

"You bought me all those gifts, didn't you?" I ask Gus, squatting down onto my knees. "Those presents on Christmas and for my birthday. They're all from you."

I put my head in my hands, my tears tumbling down my cheeks as quickly and sloppily as my letters had tumbled from the closet.

Gus wipes his eyes and speaks softly. "I didn't mean—

I just—you were stuck with me. An old man. 'Cause even your grandmother was gone at that point. It was a joy to me. It was like getting a second chance—getting another little girl, a little sister to my first. But I thought I needed to give you something else, Auggie."

I shake my head. A couple of tears drip down onto a brown paper package. "You didn't," I say, edging myself closer to him. "I just always wondered why she wouldn't come home. I don't need anything else other than you," I say, hugging him so tight that his whiskers turn to sandpaper on my cheek.

"What are we going to do now?" I wonder out loud. I finally pull my arms away from Gus's neck. "I don't have a single plan—not even a bad one. I really thought Mom would help us."

"But, Auggie," Gus says, "you just said yourself that you didn't need anything else other than what we've got here."

"This whole time, Auggie," Chuck insists, "You've been staring down that committee. Making everyone in Serendipity Place keep going, keep working on their houses. Wanting the committee to see this neighborhood in a new way. Seems to me, you've been telling that committee something, too, same as your mom told that old snake."

...52...

Gus wants to toss out the items that have fallen from the closet onto the hall floor. "Don't know why I kept them all this time, anyway," he mutters. "Guess maybe part of me was hoping that somehow, you'd break into the closet. Find all those things and know. Now—"

But I stop him. "No way, Gus," I say. "I've got the perfect idea."

❆

When we're done, Gus drives us back out to the cemetery—the one on the city limits. We carry our latest creation to the borderline—the line between staying and going. Because Gus has already gotten permission, the two of us pierce the ground right where Chuck says he and Gus spread Mom's ashes. We plant a sign, made out of the metal from the trinket boxes and the compacts and the backs of mirrors and the earrings and all the other little presents I thought I'd sent Mom.

Our sign looks like a simple stake close to the ground but turns into a bunch of stars we've cut out and welded together—dark, pot metal stars. The star at the top, though, is a bright, shiny silver. *Brighter than any star in the sky or the ones on the silver screen.* Right in the middle, Gus has welded a section with Mom's name, along with her birthday and her last day—the two dates that say "Once upon a time," and "The end."

It feels so strange, finding Mom and losing her all at once. My whole life, the idea of Mom deciding to come back has given me something to always look forward to. It makes me feel a little off balance now that I don't have it.

"She'd be real proud of that, Auggie," Gus says as he stares at the marker we've made for her. I can tell, from the way he squeezes my hand, that he's proud of it, too.

We're standing there looking at it when the Widow Hollis slowly inches her way into the cemetery, carrying a bouquet of flowers and one of those green plastic vases that can be put in the ground. She's headed toward her husband's old grave, I figure. But first, she comes to join us.

"What a beautiful sculpture," she says.

My face brightens as her word screeches into my brain.

"What did you call it?" I ask.

"A sculpture," the widow answers, like it's no big deal. "Just like all the other sculptures at your house."

209

"Wait," I say. "Sculptures?"

"Sure," she says with a shrug. "That's what everyone calls them."

"Everyone who?"

"Everyone in Serendipity Place. What have *you* been calling them?"

"Company," I admit. "I never thought of them as sculptures."

"Well, they are," she insists. "Sculptures."

I think about what a funny word that is to use for my company—they almost look like stick figures, some of them, especially the first few. And "stick figures" makes me think of kids' drawings. And that makes me think of Ms. Dillbeck's front hall. And a smiling T. Walker wandering through the maze of our figures way back at Thanksgiving.

With no warning, a new plan comes screeching right into my brain and *honks*. My entire body tingles.

"Little Sister," Gus says. "That's about the biggest smile you've ever worn."

"You bet it is," I say. "Because I just figured out how to stare down our snake for *good*."

··· 53 ···

Gus follows me outside when T. Walker Doyle shows up, fresh from New York, that weekend.

"I figure we've got so many people out here in the yard, they'll keep the sunlight from falling on the grass. Bet we won't have to mow all summer long," Gus laughs as he shakes T. Walker's hand in greeting.

"The newest ones are certainly something," T. Walker says. "Actually, though, I kind of like the story this whole yard tells. It shows how the two of you have developed as artists."

Gus opens his mouth and out pours his chicken-fried-steak laugh. "Artists," he repeats, shaking his head.

"Auggie told my aunt that all of these figures were for sale," T. Walker says, which makes Gus erupt into a new round of laughter.

"She did?" Gus says. "That's really the plan?" he teases me. He still doesn't believe it, even though he's been in on it since I first got the idea.

"Who would want one?" he asks T. Walker. "They're just our company."

T. Walker scratches his chin and fiddles with his glasses. "I do," he says. "I'd like to include some of these in my folk art museum. I think you and Auggie have a lot of natural talent."

People have called Gus a lot of things over the years, but I don't think anybody's ever called him "talented." They've sure never used that word to describe me.

I could cry—or squeal. Talented. An artist. Not a girl with white circles on her ankles or boring mud-colored skin. Auggie Jones, artist. The word grows warm inside me. For a moment, I think the word might actually, might even—shine.

"Do you know anyone else who might want one?" I ask. I hold my arms tight against my sides and cross my fingers. I cross my toes inside my sneakers.

"Sure. I know of several folk art dealers who would be interested."

"Do you think maybe they would come over?" I ask. "If we were to, say, hold a sale right here on the lawn?"

"Absolutely," he says, pulling a phone from his pocket.

Gus eyes me as he sits on the front porch.

"You're not upset about me wanting to sell our company, are you?" I ask, afraid that he might be a little hurt now that it's real—and T. Walker has agreed to help us sell our figures.

He shakes his head, draws me close to wrap an arm around my neck. "Best idea *ever*," I hear him mumble.

•••54•••

For the next week and a half, T. Walker Doyle can be seen through Ms. Dillbeck's front window, pacing with a phone to his ear. He gives me gorgeous fliers with a giant picture of our house in the middle. Gus drives me and Weird Harold through town; every time we come upon a new telephone pole, we hop out to staple a flier to it.

Because of our fliers and T. Walker's calls, a few reporters come back—some with cameras and microphones, and some from the newspaper. I straighten my back and pretend that I'm staring a mean old copperhead right in its beady little eyes.

I speak straight into the reporters' microphones and pocket recorders, telling them, "Sure, the materials we used on our house would be in the dump right now if we hadn't gotten hold of it all. But that doesn't mean it's useless. Doesn't make it garbage. We're recycling. Saving the landfill and using very little money to decorate all at the same time." I use every positive word I can think of, while Gus smiles down on me, proud.

"Ms. Byron?" I ask, bright and early the very morning after Gus and I appear on the evening news. I throw my hand in the air to get her attention, as though calling out her name wasn't enough.

"Yes?" Ms. Byron says.

"I have an announcement to make. Would it be okay to make it now?" My mouth is sticky inside, but I do my best to pretend I'm really not nervous at all. I want my announcement to sound fascinating—like the kind of thing that nobody would dare miss.

The heat of Victoria's glare hits my neck as Ms. Byron nods a yes.

I slide out of my desk. My whole body pounds like the orchestra room when the drummers are practicing by themselves.

"I would like to invite you all to an art show at my house," I say.

"Art show?" Victoria shouts. "Who are you kidding?

"Where'd she find art?" I hear Victoria mumble at Lexie. "At the dump? Underneath a bunch of rotten food?"

Lexie cringes, folds her arms over her chest, but doesn't respond.

"I'm even inviting you, Victoria," I say, acting as

though she's the one that everyone ought to feel sorry for.

"Girls," Ms. Byron warns.

"Well, when's this art show?" Victoria asks, rolling her eyes.

I smile politely and answer, "Friday. Friday night."

"Doesn't give us much time," she mutters at Lexie. "We all probably need to get tetanus shots before we even get close to her house."

Lexie doesn't laugh, though. She looks like she needs one of Ms. Byron's stomach pills.

"Friday," I repeat, and slowly walk to the back of the room. I take extra care to square my shoulders as I make my way back to my seat.

··· 55 ···

The night of the big show, I put on a yellow dress that's the color of the excitement in my belly. I pace the front hall, down the path where our old throw rug has been worn threadbare.

I stick my head in the front window and wait for everyone to start arriving. I pray, *Please, please, please . . .*

All my prayers bring are a couple of grown-ups who

act like they're only out for an evening stroll, no big deal. But they hang onto our sidewalk and stare at the front of our house a little too long for that to really be true.

Still, they won't step through our gate. They linger, pretending that they're talking about the clouds. Pretending that it's perfectly normal to retie their shoelaces four times in a row. I know that in a couple of minutes, if nobody else comes, this couple will shrug and leave, too. *Please, please let someone else show up*, I start to think. And from the way Gus's lips are wiggling, I'm pretty sure he's praying for the same thing.

Finally, one of T. Walker's friends drives up. He parks his new car on the street, and comes right through our front gate, like T. Walker did when I met him. A few more of T. Walker's friends show up soon after—I recognize them by their church slacks—and they all start to wander through our front yard like they're really in a big department store, looking at the things on the racks that are for sale.

That makes the original two curiosity-seekers brave. They quit pretending they're just wandering by. They come through our gate, too.

Before long, it's a whole stampede of feet and cars.

 216

Lexie shows up with the Coles—Victoria and her father—who are wearing identical scowls. The rest of the suits that have been at our City Hall meetings show up, too. I recognize the faces of the entire House Beautification Committee.

Our yard swarms with suits and worn-out T-shirts alike. Ms. Dillbeck and the Widow Hollis and Mrs. Pike and Irma Jean and Chuck Taylor and Mr. Gutz-Chong and Weird Harold and his dad all start to wander through. Ms. Byron even comes. So does Mick from McGunn's, his hairy arms exposed by his white T-shirt. He eyes our sculptures an extra-long time, smiling and pointing at what we've done with some of the things we used to bring to his junkyard.

Our front yard is so full, people can hardly find a place to stand. I think Gus will have to tie me down, I'm so happy.

"Just a minute now, Little Sister," Gus says. "Hang on just a little longer."

Gus and I fidget in the front window. Waiting for the perfect moment to finally make an appearance.

A reporter from a news station arrives with her camera crew, followed by a second reporter from another station. The crowd continues to swell, spilling onto the sidewalk and into the street, as the two reporters hold their mics beneath their mouths, speaking as they look straight into their cameras.

A black-and-white police car rolls to a stop, and an officer emerges, raising a bullhorn and barking at the crowd that he's there to control them. To remind them they're on private property.

When even the mayor shows up, flashing his smile at everyone in the yard, I ask, "Now, Gus? Can we go *now*?"

"Now, Little Sister," Gus agrees, and we bolt for the door.

"Where's the big art show?" Victoria shouts as soon as she sees us. "You promised art!"

"It's right here," T. Walker says, pointing at our metal figures.

"This isn't art," Victoria says. "It's trash." Her father and some of the suits they're with snicker and nod in agreement.

"It most certainly is art," T. Walker argues. "And I'm not the only one who thinks so." He points at the rest of his friends. "These are also art dealers. Folk art dealers, to be exact. They agree that this is the greatest example of folk art any of us have seen in a long time."

"But they're ugly!" Victoria shouts.

"I happen to think they're really quite beautiful," T.

Walker says. "These sculptures are extremely imaginative and magnificently made."

T. Walker points to five sculptures right off and pulls his wallet out of his pocket. He hands me a fat wad of money.

"I'll take these four," another dealer says as he hands me a stack of bills.

All of T. Walker's friends buy our sculptures. Some take one or two; some point to the roof and say, "I'd like that sunflower up there." Or, "Is the butterfly up for grabs?" Another shouts, "Don't break the bouquet apart—I want the whole thing!"

A frenzy of buying starts in, with dealers carefully lifting our sculptures and carrying them off to their cars.

"Wait—you can't be serious!" Victoria tries, but no one listens.

I have so much money, I have to use my yellow dress as a kind of basket to hold it all. Mixed in with the green bills, I've also got checks written out to Gus. I've never seen so much money all piled up in the same place in my life—the sight of it makes my heels bob up and down and Gus explode with that hearty chicken-fried-steak laugh of his.

"Here," I say, walking up to Mr. Cole. "This is surely enough to take care of our fines. I bet that'll also take

care of the fines for Mrs. Pike's swing set, the Bradshaws' and the Widow Hollis's roofs, Ms. Dillbeck's
porch, and Mrs. Shoemacker's screens."

Mr. Cole starts counting the money furiously.

"Is it really enough, sir?" the police officer asks.

Mr. Cole's face tumbles a bit as he mutters, "It—it
is."

Gus cheers behind me. So do T. Walker and a couple
of his art friends.

Those cheers get inside me, fill me with bravery.

"I'm telling you, once and for all, Victoria," I start, in
a way that makes the real, live breathing crowd grow
just as quiet as the metal one. "You might want to do
something important, but you can't bulldoze people's
houses because they're in your way."

Victoria crosses her arms over her chest and juts her
chin out, putting on the kind of pout that finds poor
losers after a game.

I realize one of the reporters has put a microphone
under my mouth. I lean closer to it to say, "You want
to know what this committee's *really* about? This committee wants to get our homes for next to nothing. But
it's not right to toss an entire neighborhood out to turn
their homes into a community center.

"It won't happen, Victoria. Not as long as Gus and

I have anything to do with it. You can go on and slap your unfair fines on us. Go ahead and slap them on everyone else in the neighborhood, too. We'll just sell some more sculptures to pay them off."

Victoria backs away from me as her dad pushes his way toward the microphone, trying to calm the growling crowd with words like "friends," and "reevaluation," and "miscommunication."

But it seems a little too late for words like that. Because other words—*art* and *beautiful*—have suddenly made everyone in our yard tilt their heads and look at our house in a new way. And my words—*bulldoze* and *fines* and *unfair*—have made one man behind me mutter, "Seems to me, the House Beautification Committee has stepped way out of bounds."

Other heads bob in agreement. "This committee's working *against* the people in this town, not *for* them," another says.

The mayor pushes his way up toward the TV news teams. As he walks, the crowd gets noisier and noisier, shouting protests.

"We're going to—no one will lose their home— I'll—" the mayor tries, but no one's listening. Not to him, anyway. Not now.

As Victoria and I continue to glare at each other, it

221

feels like suddenly, the whole world's no longer against me and Gus. It's like everything I've been fighting is now deciding to wrap its arms around me and hug me.

A voice from the far side of the yard says, "I'm not an art dealer, but could I buy one of your sculptures?"

"Yeah," comes another shout. "I want one, too!"

"I want one for Dickerson!" Ms. Byron calls out. "To highlight student talent!" She's smiling at me, not eating any stomach pills at all.

"Are some of those sculptures really made out of old playground equipment from Montgomery?" one of the suits standing next to Mr. Cole asks.

Mr. Cole frowns at his fellow committee member. "What are you doing?" he hisses.

But the suit waves him away. "I'd do anything to get a sculpture made out of a Montgomery swing," he admits. "It'd be like getting a little piece of my child-hood back!"

Victoria shrinks as the man hurries to pick out a sculpture before they're all spoken for.

"Wait!" Weird Harold shouts as another House Beau-tification member reaches for the girl with the beret and the palette. "You can't have that one," he goes on, smiling from underneath a cap that says EYE OF THE BEHOLDER.

222

"Why not, son?" the man asks, looking like Harold's just slapped his hand.

"She's an artist," Harold explains, staring right at me. "That one has to stay."

I'm still beaming when a clickety-clack sound explodes behind me. At first, I think it must be someone leaving, their hard-soled shoes clopping away. But when I turn, I see that the Reverend Chuck Taylor is clapping. And Weird Harold is whistling through his teeth, clapping, too, and shouting, "Way to go, Auggie!"

Soon, everyone is clapping—applauding for Gus and for me, Auggie Jones.

 · · · 56 · · ·

After the art show, Gus and I go to work, making maybe fifty more people to replace the ones we sold. By now, late in the summer, girls jump hopscotch squares on our front walk. Boys play with model airplanes. A couple kisses right out in the open. A boy squats down to tie his shoelace. A full-grown man walks his dog. A bashful girl stares at her feet, her hands tucked behind her back. A woman paints her toenails.

Every time we make a new sculpture, it's a little bit better than the last. I can't wait to see what we'll be making a year from now—two years, even. Maybe ten.

I figure by the time I'm as old as Gus, I'll be making sculptures that are so lifelike, guys passing by on the street will stop and ask one of them for the time, then stomp off in a huff when they don't get an answer right back.

"Come on, Gus!" I shout as I explode through the front door, because I can't wait to get to McGunn's. I'm halfway down the front walk when I hear the sign on our gate rattle.

Gus didn't much like the idea of the sign at first. Especially since what I wanted to put on it had hurt him so much back when Victoria first said it: "The Junk-tion of Sunshine and Lucky."

But I insisted we spell it right: THE JUNCTION OF SUN-SHINE AND LUCKY. "After all, we do live on the corner," I reasoned. "And I want to take that awful name Victoria gave us and turn it into something pretty, just like we take anything broken or ugly and make it in to something T. Walker wants to put in his museum."

Since we hung that sign up, the name has really caught on. These days, when a family on vacation or somebody on business asks a waitress or a gas station

worker what there is to do for fun, they're always told, "You can't leave town without visiting The Junction of Sunshine and Lucky." Three times out of four, one of those visitors winds up buying a sculpture right out of our yard.

It's not a stranger on vacation who has just opened our gate, though. It's Lexie.

She drags her feet as she walks toward me, shuffling along like she's been sent to the principal's office. I'm beginning to wonder if she needs me to say something first when she blurts, "I wanted you to have this," and pushes a frame into my hands.

It's a photo of Mom's billboard.

"They're peeling her old picture off," Lexie says softly. "It's going to be an ad for the new community center. The one they're going to put in Montgomery."

"I heard," I say, hugging the frame to my chest.

"So you still have something to wish on," Lexie says, pointing at the picture.

I realize that her hair has grown out to her chin, and that she's got it pulled up on one side of her head with a little barrette. Her face is getting a glistening coat of sweat on it, too—and the way she fidgets tells me it's not because of the heat.

"You were right about Victoria," she admits. "All of it."

225

"Yeah," I mutter, and as we stare at each other, I start to make a new wish. Because I don't want Lexie to feel bad anymore.

"Auggie!" Irma Jean shouts as she races down her front steps. "You and Gus are going to McGunn's, right?"

Just as Lexie starts to back away, I wrap an arm around her neck. "We're *all* going," I say, making Lexie flash a smile as bright as a piece of metal glistening in the sun. That smile says my wish just came true.

We cram ourselves into the cab of Old Glory. "You girls are giggling louder than a whole zoo of hyenas," Gus says as he steers us down Sunshine, right past the arch we gave back to Mrs. Shoemacker. I finally did figure out how to fix it. Now, it sits at the edge of her front walk, completely covered in leaves cut from metal flashing and tied on loosely with green wire. When the breeze hits, the leaves rattle, promising that the arch will never have just one vine on it again. The noise it makes always tugs a laugh from Mr. Shoemacker—who's finally back home—every time he picks up the paper or the mail.

As we head toward Joy, I think of all the other projects in the works—plans we have for our neighbors in Serendipity Place. Because not all of our sculptures go in the yard. A good number go straight to T. Walker Doyle, who sells them off and sends checks back to Gus. Sure, we've used those checks to buy groceries and a few new dresses and even a better TV and a new Frigidaire. But we have enough to put some aside, too.

Now that the mayor has forgiven the fines—which most folks in town swore weren't exactly on the up and up, anyway—the entirety of our put-aside money is going to help everyone else in Serendipity Place fix up their houses in ways that say something about the people who live inside: the Shoemackers are getting a new front door with a window right in the middle, so everyone can see the warm and welcoming inside of their house. Ms. Dillbeck wants awnings on her two front windows—black ones, that look like eyelashes— to emphasize the way I've told her that her porch looks like a mouth smiling. And the Pikes plan on painting their house two shades of yellow, one much darker than the other, the same way a daffodil is a darker orangey-yellow in the center. Because daffodils show up in the spring, and spring is for new babies—that's what Mrs. Pike says, anyway—and that sums them up completely.

Gus slows down in front of the Bradshaw place,

beside one of our metal sculptures—a farmer with a small motor that lets him tip a watering can to let some cellophane that looks an awful lot like water roll out, then roll back in. The farmer stands proudly right in the middle of the gardens that grow once again in their front yard. Harold grins beneath a hat that reads HOME SWEET HOME.

Old Glory rattles to a stop, and Harold piles in, too. We're all so squashed, it's a little hard to breathe. Our voices get especially loud inside Old Glory as we drive by Hopewell, and I smile at the yellow construction equipment parked by the curb.

After the mayor broke up the House Beautification Committee, jars started popping up next to cash registers all over town. People were happy to plunk their change inside, because *old building* and *eyesore* were suddenly words that didn't fit together anymore. So Chuck got enough to start rebuilding Hopewell after all.

At McGunn's, the doors open and we tumble out. We race straight for the donation bins that are set up at the edge of the junkyard—bins where anyone can drop off their used items for me and Gus to use on our sculptures.

"You guys got a ton of stuff!" Harold shouts, dropping

to his knees as he digs through the contents. "A brake drum! A carburetor! Buttons from a Coke machine!" He always knows what every broken piece of machinery is in our donation bin. Knowing what the pieces did in their old lives helps give me new ideas for how I can use them in sculptures or even whirligigs, which is the fancy word T. Walker uses to describe some pieces Gus and I make that are powered by motors or twirl in the wind.

"Front-row seats," Mick says, reaching out with a hair-covered arm to pat an old refrigerator, stretched out on its side.

The girls and I climb on top of the fridge. When Gus brings us Cokes from the McGunn soda machine, I gulp mine down so fast, the cold puts an icy stripe straight through my head.

"School starts in a couple of weeks, doesn't it?" Mick asks. "Any first-day jitters?"

"A few," Lexie admits, because here we are, looking another school year square in the face. Middle school, this time. "Lockers," she grimaces.

"But I bet you'll have an incredible new hairdo," I say, nudging her.

"You won't *believe* what I made to wear on the first day of middle school," Irma Jean announces, her voice so loud and excited that we all laugh at the same time—me and Gus and Irma Jean and Harold and Lexie. The tones in our laughter blend into the world's most beautiful piano chord—so big, it would take two hands to play all the notes at once.

I watch as Gus detaches an old Pontiac from his winch, listening to the happy voices and the clink of items as Harold digs deeper into the donation box. Plans for new sculptures start swirling—so many of them, I can hardly keep up with them all. I tell myself to only focus on three—the most important three. The three that feel the closest to me:

1. A girl made out of steel because she's so tough—and she's staring down a hose painted up like a copperhead snake.

2. A girl who is so special, she has a picture frame for a face.

3. A girl who is reaching for a star.

Author's Note

When I was Auggie's age, I started going to farm auctions with my folks. I grew up in Missouri (again, just like Auggie), in a town that was a pretty even mix of city life and rural surroundings. My childhood house, located in the third biggest city in the state, was also just a stone's throw from a field marked off with barbed wire! We never really had to go far to find auctions on old farmland.

I mostly spent those auctions under enormous shade trees with piles of books. Every once in a while, I'd take a break from reading to crowd-watch. The grown-ups who came to those auctions ran the gamut. They were antique dealers looking for pieces to sell, or they were collectors looking to add items to their displays, or they were rugged men in overalls who wanted cheap supplies for their own farms. Looking back now, it seems as though those dealers and collectors became the basis for T. Walker, and those crafty old farming guys who'd spent their lives in Missouri were the basis for Gus.

Many of the treasures at farm auctions were handmade, using reinvented materials. Some had been created out of necessity: Hand-forged tools made from pieces of old machinery. Quilts with intricate patterns, sewn from old scraps of clothing. Primitive-looking furniture made from old wooden crates. Other items were used as decoration, such as small wooden dresser knickknacks made from cigar boxes, or framed needlework on old burlap feed sacks.

The beginning of Auggie's story came to me years after my first farm auction. Actually, I didn't get the idea for a *story* as much as I got an idea for *characters*, and the book spiraled out after that.

The first person I saw was Gus. I saw him as clearly as I've seen any real person I've ever met in life. It was as if I were looking through Auggie's eyes, straight at her grampa. I knew I had to write about the kind of people who created those unique, handmade items I'd been finding at auction. But I wanted my characters to make bigger items, wilder items. Full-blown sculptures.

My favorite part of Auggie's story is the way she stumbles upon her talent, in the same way my family once stumbled upon items for sale at auction. I think that's so true in life. Everybody in this world has a shine, just like Auggie. But Auggie's original goal was to spruce up her house. She never would have guessed, in the beginning, that it would lead to her becoming a folk artist. You never know when your shine will appear… and sometimes, it takes a creative eye to recognize it.

Acknowledgments

Auggie's story has been with me for years—the journey from first sentence to finished book has been a long and winding one—and I'm so grateful to have shared that journey with such a passionate group:

Thanks to my ever-enthusiastic agent, Deborah Warren; to my editor, Nancy Conescu, for making sure this book is the absolute best it could be; to copyeditor Rosanne Lauer for her sharp eye and fine-toothed comb; to Lindsey Andrews for a fantastic cover concept; and to everyone at Dial Books for giving Auggie a "home."

Thanks to my mom, who read every single draft of *The Junction of Sunshine and Lucky*, and to my brother, John, who's never missed an author event.

. . . And I want to give a special thanks to you, my reader, who's holding this book in your hands . . .

About the Author

Holly Schindler knew, when she was a little girl writing stories at her child-sized rolltop desk, that she wanted to be an author. Although her desk is bigger and she no longer delivers her stories by Big Wheel, Holly still loves writing for children of all ages. She can be found working on her next novel for young readers at her home in Springfield, Missouri. She can also be reached online at hollyschindler.com.